From the Ashes

Tennille Jo Mortensen

ISBN 978-1-7370726-3-8

Dedication

For my daughters: May you always see God's hand in your life.

For Lois and Ralph, whose love, faith,
and endurance is an inspiration

Overture

We all come to that intersection – the intersection where our hopes, dreams, and expectations collide with reality head on. We may not know the exact day or time, but it is an inevitable road we must all cross. There will be fatalities, and we will be forced to bury some of those hopes and dreams we've had since childhood. The question is how long will we mourn? How long will we linger on the past before embracing the unexpected future that lies ahead of us? Here is our defining moment. Will we imprison ourselves with those broken dreams, staring out of the cage of what might have been, or will we pave a new way – one step at a time – opening our hearts to new possibilities? Which path will you choose?

Chance Encounters

Ainsley Nelson stared at the computer for what seemed like the millionth hour. She was putting the final touches on her updated resume, amazed that the last nine years of her life had been reduced to a single sheet of paper that listed her major accomplishments: a Bachelor of Business Administration degree in accounting, a Master of Business Administration degree, and a Certified Public Accountant certification. Would it be enough to differentiate her from the rest of the eager job applicants?

Seeing no mistakes, she opened her e-mail and selected the folder where she had already saved a draft of her cover letter in e-mail form as requested on the application. She had read her resume at least twenty times, checking and re-checking for errors, but she decided to read it once more, just in case.

Had she added a more intimate description of herself to her resume to further distinguish herself from the pack, it may have read something like this:

1

PHYSICAL DESCRIPTION
- ❖ Thick, straight, waist-length wheat blonde hair
- ❖ Dark green eyes
- ❖ 5 ft. 8 in. tall, approximately 150 lbs.

HOBBIES & INTERESTS
- ❖ Scrapbooking and photography
- ❖ Drawing (received an art minor with bachelor's degree)
- ❖ Hanging out with friends
- ❖ Reading and watching movies
- ❖ Spending time on the coast
- ❖ Enjoying Ben & Jerry's Ice Cream

OTHER
- ❖ Marital Status: Single
- ❖ Age: 28
- ❖ Religion: The Church of Jesus Christ of Latter-day Saints
- ❖ Best Friend: Deedra Morris

Perhaps adding personal details would merely blend her into the background since there wasn't anything too exciting about her extracurricular life. In reality, she was just an ordinary woman living an ordinary life. She would have to rely on her professional qualifications.

She attached her resume, hesitated, and finally clicked on the send button. She took a deep breath, exhaling slowly. *Here's to my future*, she thought as the trepidation began to rise from somewhere within like carbonation bubbles surfacing in a freshly opened soft drink can. She wasn't sure she was ready to move on from the university, which had been her "home" for the last nine years, but she had no choice.

After graduating with her MBA, she had been offered a temporary accounting position in the Grants and Contracts Department at Portland State

University, where she had previously been working as a graduate assistant. The job was supposed to last only one year, but each year for three years, the funding had been renewed until now. One month ago, she had been given notice that her position would be eliminated due to the current budget crisis, and she had found little luck in her job search efforts. Her most recent application was submitted to the City of Portland, which had advertised an opening for a financial analyst position with the Grants Administration Staff. She was banking on her extensive experience working in the governmental accounting sector to boost her chances of at least securing an interview with the city. Unfortunately, it was out of her hands now, so she shut her laptop with a sigh and tried to get some sleep.

A week later, she received an e-mail advising her she had an interview with the city the following day at 10:00 am. Relief rushed over her. She had passed the first hurdle, although her track record for interviews was less than stellar. *Just one more interview*, she tried to encourage herself.

Early the next morning, Ainsley stopped by the dry cleaners to pick up her one and only dress suit. She hung it in the back seat of the white Ford Contour her parents had bought for her when she graduated from high school. It was used then, but it still drove like a dream and smelled like a new car to her. Her mind was buzzing with possible interview questions as she made a growing mental checklist of tasks she needed to complete. Her brain was on autopilot as far as backing out of her parking space was concerned, until she heard a crunching sound as the car came to an abrupt halt. Her heart sprinted the 100-

meter dash as she glanced into her rearview mirror only to confirm that she had just backed into a silver Honda SUV. Her mind was drawing a blank as she tried to recall whether or not she had checked her blind spot. She couldn't see if there was any damage from where she was sitting. With shaking hands, she reached for her insurance information. There was no use delaying the inevitable. Her door creaked as it opened as though groaning in pain as she stepped into the cold chill of the February morning. She didn't even have both shoes on the pavement before the other driver was standing in front of her, blocking her path confrontationally.

"What the devil are you doing, lady?" he shouted as if he were using a megaphone to announce to the world that she was a worthless piece of scum. Several profanities escaped his angry lips in his next breath. Her mouth suddenly went so dry she thought tumbleweed might roll out if she tried to speak. The man continued to berate her in front of a gathering crowd. Her face was flushed with embarrassment, and she could feel sweat beading on her forehead in the heat of the moment. Her blood was boiling with rage at this man's onslaught, but she knew a confrontation would do little to quiet his temper. It would only add gasoline to the fire that was already burning out of control. Though her pulse was still racing through her veins at a pace set to win an Olympic medal sprint, she appeared to all spectators as calm as a lake on a clear, breezeless day.

"I mean seriously! I didn't know the DMV was issuing licenses to the blind now," the man continued his ranting as Ainsley tried to maintain direct eye contact with him. Had she merely passed him on an aisle in the supermarket, she may have considered him handsome enough for a second look. He was slightly taller than her with disheveled, coal-black hair that curled in just the right places. His deep brown eyes looked like liquid chocolate trapped in a sea of white. His olive skin was nicely stretched over smooth, though slightly neglected, muscles.

While he was fit, his six-pack had long since faded. Had she not been the black silhouette of his target practice, she may have noticed, but she did not. She saw only two, large, black holes as she stared into his cold eyes – two empty spaces, left void by his anger toward her.

"Well," he demanded, "what do you have to say for yourself?" It was the first time he had stopped long enough for her to speak. In fact, in his five-minute tirade, she wasn't even sure he had stopped to take a breath.

"I...I'm sorry," she stammered, but quickly regained her composure so as not to give him the feeling that he had gained the upper hand by belittling her in front of the now dwindling crowd. She had been slightly disappointed that no one had come to her aid, but then again, they were only there for the show. Who needs reality TV when there's a showdown in the dry cleaner's parking lot? She wouldn't have been surprised if someone were recording the unfortunate event and streaming it live as she fumbled for her words.

"Oh, you're sorry? Like that's going to make all this go away," he began to launch into another string of expletives, but this time she interrupted.

"You've made your feelings crystal clear to the entire strip mall, sir," she said sternly. "Right now, all we need to do is exchange insurance information." She began writing her information down on a scrap of paper.

"No, what I need to do is call the police to have you arrested," he threatened in a low tone. She said nothing but moved to the rear of her car to survey the damage. Her taillight was broken, and the frame of the car was dented in one spot. His vehicle had only a small dent in the rear passenger side door. She took her cell phone out to take a picture of the damage to both vehicles. It was clear that she had backed into him, so she didn't press him for his insurance information. She merely handed him her information as she said, "The police won't file a report because this is a private parking lot, so there's really no need to call them since no one was injured."

"I see. I'm dealing with a professional. I bet you're on a first name basis with the officers on this beat," he fumed. She stared at him disdainfully in utter disbelief but felt that the comment didn't warrant acknowledgement.

"All I need is your name and number," she noted, gripping her pen tightly to quell the new tremors that were surging through her hands.

"Wow," he responded dryly, "I get it. This is some pathetic attempt to pick up on poor unsuspecting guys who drive nice vehicles. Go to hell!" He seethed as he ripped the paper upon which she had written her insurance information out of her hand. He briskly walked to the driver's side of his vehicle and scrambled inside, slamming the door as hard as he could before he sped off.

"Same to you," she muttered under her breath as she jotted down his license plate number before he disappeared from sight. She slipped back into her car and burst into tears as soon as she shut the door. *He must be a professional jerk*, she thought to herself. This was clearly not the way she wanted to start off the most important day of her life – a day upon which her entire future hinged. She tried to push the incident out of her head so she could drive somewhat competently back to her apartment.

None of her roommates were home when she returned, for which she was grateful. She didn't want to have to relive the experience just yet. As she sat down, her cell phone rang. She hesitantly looked at the caller id, hoping the caller wasn't Mr. Road Rage jumping in the ring for round two. She wasn't sure she could take much more.

It was her mom. She answered the phone, but the moment she heard the familiar voice on the other end, she could feel the tears burning their way to the surface again, desperate to be released. Her mom always called at precisely the right moment, and Ainsley launched into an explanation of her traumatic morning. Even though she was twenty-eight, she swallowed her mom's reassurances as if they were gulps of sweet lemonade on a hot summer day.

"Thanks, Mom," Ainsley said, "I'm glad you called."

"I actually called to wish you luck on your interview. I still wish you'd move back here, but I know you really want to find your own way in the world. Just be sure you feel good about staying there. Don't just take the first job that comes along," her mom advised.

"Mom, please," Ainsley protested. "You know there's nowhere to work out there. Besides, I'm comfortable here. I've been here for nine years now. This is my home. And about the job – this is my fifth interview – I haven't received one offer yet. I'm getting more than a little desperate. I'm going to have to take the first job that comes along. Companies aren't really bending over backwards to hire me."

"I know, honey," her mom replied with resignation in her tone. "By the way, you let me know if that guy starts harassing you at all. I hate that you had to give your phone number to him, and now he knows where you live as well."

"Gee, thanks, Mom. I hadn't thought about that until you mentioned it. It's not like I don't already have enough to worry about," Ainsley was getting a little annoyed with the direction of the conversation. She just hoped her mom didn't end it with her typical, *"If only you could find someone to settle down with. He could take care of you."*

"I'm sorry. I'm sure nothing will come of it dear. I just wish you could find someone –" Ainsley didn't wait for her to finish.

"Mom, I can take care of myself!" she interrupted, exasperated.

"Okay. Okay. Good luck with your interview. We love you," she said, letting the issue drop. The topic was like a pesky fly that would never die. No matter how hard she swatted it to death, someone always resurrected it at least once a month, and it was usually her mother.

"Love you too, Mom. Bye," she replied as she pushed the end button on her phone. The display lit up, revealing the time to be 9:30. She was going to be late for her interview. She quickly changed her clothes and shoes, re-applied her make-up to cover up her tear-stained cheeks and washed-out mascara, and darted out the door. *Why can't anything go according to plan?* She complained to herself as she pulled into a parking space. She paused to take a deep breath before exiting her vehicle and happened to glance down at her shoes. To her horror, she realized that in her hurry to get out the door, she had put on mismatched shoes. They were the same color and mostly the same style, but the square heel was two inches higher on her left shoe. *What else could possibly go wrong?* she thought as she slinked into the building, walking as one does with heels of different sizes on each foot. She checked in at the receptionist's desk and nervously sat down to wait. The minutes ticked by ever so slowly as the large clock above her head loudly announced each passing second.

"Ms. Nelson, we're ready for you," a man beckoned to her from a conference room. She rose, trying to appear confident, despite her awkward gait. Five people were seated on one side of a table with an empty chair pulled out on the opposite side. A pitcher of water sat in the middle of the table with several glasses, indicating that the group was to be interviewing several candidates that morning, though she appeared to be the first. She felt as though she were sitting before a parole board preparing to plead her case for freedom. These five people could change the outcome of her entire life. She sat in the chair and smiled at the man who had called her in. He introduced himself as Jedidiah Corbett. He appeared to be the eldest of the five, with a balding head and a salt and pepper mustache. He then introduced the other four interviewers, at whom Ainsley had barely glanced. Ainsley's blood froze in her veins as her eyes settled on the man seated at the end of the table.

"This is Brandt Cragun," Mr. Corbett announced. "He's the senior financial analyst on the budget and financial planning staff. The person who fills this position will work closely with his department on a special project for the first few months after the position is filled, so we invited him to sit in on the interview as well." Ainsley didn't know him as Brandt Cragun because he had never given her his name – she referred to him as Mr. Road Rage. His eyes narrowed as silent recognition crossed her face, draining all the color from it at once.

"Are you feeling okay, Ms. Nelson?" Mr. Corbett asked.

So much for this job, she thought as she fidgeted in her seat. Her executioner had just been named, and the sneer on his face told her that he was more than willing to decapitate her from a future at the city with his freshly sharpened guillotine. Worse, he appeared to be staring directly at her mismatched shoes. While her mind was quietly killing her hope, her voice defiantly broke through its grip to reply to Mr. Corbett's question.

"Yes. I'm fine . . . thank you."

"Let me pour you a glass of water before we get started at least," he offered.

"That would be great. Thanks." She took a small sip of the water and relaxed as the cool liquid trickled down her throat.

"Very well then. Shall we get started?" Mr. Corbett asked, and with a nod from Ainsley, the interview commenced. Ainsley answered the questions knowledgably and confidently, while avoiding any glances in Brandt Cragun's direction. Although several times, she caught sight of him out of the corner of her eye lifting his arm to jot down notes on his clipboard. She was quite surprised that he asked no questions himself.

Before the interview concluded, Mr. Corbett turned to him and asked, "Do you have any questions for Ms. Nelson?" Brandt merely shook his head smugly, never speaking throughout the entire interview.

"Well, then. It looks like we're finished here. It was a pleasure meeting you. We hope to come to a decision by early next week," Mr. Corbett said as he rose to shake Ainsley's hand from across the table. She expressed her thanks and escorted herself to the door, walking gracelessly across the carpeted floor. While she wished to exit the building immediately, she had to stop by the restroom first. When she came out, she found herself standing face to face with Brandt Cragun, who had exited the men's restroom just opposite her.

"Nice shoes," he said with a smirk as he turned to walk back toward the conference room. She felt her face turn red like the rising temperature on a candy thermometer when subjected to intense heat. She had the sudden urge to take a shoe off and throw it directly at his head, but instead she rushed in the opposite direction of his haughty, spiteful saunter. Her vision blurred as a warning of the rising flood in her eyes. She drove home trying to use her eyelids as windshield wipers so she could see through the torrents of tears. When she walked into the apartment, her roommate and best friend, Deedra, greeted her.

"Hey Zee! How was the int –" she stopped short when she looked up to see Ainsley's tear-stained face.

"Oh, the interview was fine," she said flatly.

"But. . ." Deedra prodded. Ainsley launched into a retelling of the entire story, sparing no detail.

"Wow. I don't even know what to say, and few things leave me speechless." She leaned over to give Ainsley a hug. "I think this is grounds for Ben and Jerry's Oatmeal Cookie Crunch ice cream. C'mon . . . let's go."

"I would," replied Ainsley, "but I'm afraid I'll run into him again."

"Well – I'll be back in a few then," Deedra grabbed her car keys and headed out the door just as Ainsley's phone rang. It was her mom. Ainsley retold the unbelievable tale of her second encounter with the devil himself. When she hung up, she called the insurance company and then the repair shop. Deedra was back in half an hour, and the rest of the afternoon was spent drowning her bad day of chance encounters in melting ice cream.

Changes

"Zee! Your phone is ringing!" called Deedra from the kitchen a week later. Ainsley jumped off her bed, running to the living room to snatch up her cell phone before it went to voice mail. She had jumped at the sound of the ringer every time she heard it over the past week, praying it was the call she was waiting for – a call offering her the job with the City of Portland, even if she had to work alongside Mr. Road Rage. She had already received two rejection letters from positions for which she had interviewed two weeks prior.

"Hello," she said nervously.

"Is this Ainsley Nelson?" the familiar voice asked.

"Yes, yes, it is," she answered eagerly.

"This is Jedidiah Corbett from the City of Portland. I'm calling to offer you the position for which you applied as a financial analyst in grants administration, if you're still interested," he said casually.

"I am very interested. Thank you so much, Mr. Corbett," she could hardly contain her excitement.

"Glad to hear it," he said. "Congratulations! We'd like you to start first thing on Monday morning. Report to the office at 8:00 am and check in with the receptionist. She'll show you to human resources so you can fill out all your paperwork."

"Thank you again. We'll see you on Monday," she added, hanging up her phone and slumping onto the couch in a wave of relief.

"What's up?" Deedra asked, coming around the corner.

"I got the job!" Ainsley exclaimed excitedly, "I start on Monday." A perma-grin stretched across her face as Deedra began singing, "There's going to be a party tonight, a PARTY tonight, you know!" They danced around the apartment jubilantly singing at the top of their lungs. When they collapsed on Ainsley's bed at the conclusion of their celebratory song and dance, Deedra said, "I'm so relieved, now I can tell you my news."

"What news?" Ainsley asked, her heart sinking with fear that Deedra was going to tell her that Devon had popped the question. Deedra and Devon had been dating off and on for the last year, but Ainsley hadn't thought it was that serious.

Ainsley had always considered Deedra to be beautiful with her short, black ultra-curly hair, her light brown skin, and dark brown eyes. She was three years younger than Ainsley, but they had been best friends ever since Deedra's freshmen year of college when she had moved into Ainsley's apartment. Deedra was high-spirited, sassy, fun, and spiritual to top it all off, and Ainsley was sure that marriage would steal away her best friend before too much longer. It was inevitable. Ainsley masked her rising fear as she turned her head toward Deedra.

"We're moving!" she declared.

"What?" That was a far cry from an engagement announcement.

"One of my dad's rentals just became available, and I told him we'd take it since our lease is up at the end of the month anyway," she explained. Deedra's father, a prominent neurosurgeon, had several rental properties he used as real estate investments. All of them were houses in newer developments throughout the Portland area.

"What about Liza and Shauna?" Ainsley asked about the other two roommates who shared the apartment.

"Shauna just got the job in Phoenix, so she's moving out at the end of the month anyway. Liza's on board with the move, and my little sister, Corrin, will be our fourth roommate. And the greatest part is that it's a four-bedroom house, so we can each have our own rooms."

"But what about rent? You know I can't afford to pay any more than I pay here," Deedra rolled her eyes at Ainsley's remark.

"C'mon, Zee! Your rent will stay the same. My dad's not going to try to make money off me and my friends. Besides, with my sister and I both moving in, it's a moot point. He'd rather pay for something he'll own rather than throwing the money away in renting two apartments."

"It sounds like you've already got everything worked out. A room of my own sounds more than a little enticing after living with you and all your slobby habits," she joked.

Ainsley's first day of work came and went without consequence. She completed paperwork, met her co-workers, of whom Brandt Cragun was not among, and was shown to her cubicle. In fact, the first week was great. She attended training sessions to familiarize herself with the software and programs the city used, and she was briefed on the grants and her specific responsibilities as a financial analyst. She was hoping Mr. Corbett had forgotten about the project with Brandt Cragun that he had mentioned during the interview. Two weeks into the job, however, Mr. Corbett came to her cubicle.

"Ainsley, today you're going to start on the integration project with Brandt," he said matter-of-factly. Ainsley suddenly felt nauseous. She was going to be thrown into the wolf's den with no warning and no time to prepare.

"Yes, sir," she acknowledged.

"If you'll follow me, I'll show you where to go." He waited for her to grab a notebook and a pen, and she followed him reluctantly. Although dreading her first professional encounter with Mr. Road Rage, she was going to have to make the best of the situation since she had no choice but to work with him. Mr. Corbett led her to a small office situated at the end of a long hall on the basement level of the building. The room was partitioned into two workspaces. The one on the left housed Brandt Cragun. His cubicle was organized and clean with few personal belongings on open display. He had only one picture on his desk of a little girl who appeared to be younger than 12. She had the same brown eyes as Brandt, but her hair was blonde – a few shades lighter than Ainsley's. The girl's hair fell to her shoulders in big bouncy curls.

"Jed," Brandt rose to shake Mr. Corbett's hand, "it's good to see you this morning."

"You remember Ainsley Nelson?" Jed asked, and Brandt tilted his head slightly forward in acknowledgement, though his eyes never looked in Ainsley's direction.

"I want you two to get started on the project as we discussed last week. I

15

trust you'll fill her in on all the details," Jed instructed as he turned to leave the room.

"Oh, and Ainsley," he added, pausing in the doorway, "this will be your new home until the project is implemented. Then, you'll resume your duties in grants. For now, you'll live and breathe this project, and you can use the other desk in here." Jed left the room, his brisk footsteps echoing down the hallway.

"Well," Brandt began, "let's just hope you're more competent in your work skills than you are in your driving and dressing skills, or this is going to make for one long project." His meaning did not go unnoticed: Their work relationship was to be adversarial, and her work environment was proving to be far from pleasant. Apparently, there was no concept of water under the bridge with this man.

"Yeah, it's nice to be working with you too," she muttered under her breath, her eyebrows knit in disdain.

"By the way," he said coolly, "I hope you negotiated for a higher base salary before you accepted the job offer. You're going to need it to pay for your higher insurance premium, unless of course they've suspended your license by now," he jabbed again.

"I appreciate your concern, Mr. Cragun, but I'm more than capable of taking care of my own affairs without your unsolicited advice," she retorted. "Now, shall we get started?"

"I suppose we shall," he mimicked. He apparently couldn't help but be a complete jerk, so she felt obligated to set him straight on her position.

"Contrary to your erroneous assumptions about me, which I might add were based on isolated instances and taken entirely out of context, I am very competent in my field; otherwise, I would not have been offered this position. And I will give you my personal assurance that I will devote my entire life to this project if it ensures that my interaction with the likes of you is as brief as possible," she declared as she pulled a chair to the front of his desk. He chuckled faintly under his breath, but just as quickly put on his business-as-usual face. *Spiteful creature!* Ainsley seethed inaudibly. He began explaining the project as soon as she sat down as though she hadn't spoken at all – as if her retort hadn't left the faintest blemish on his super ego.

She took detailed notes as he spoke, looking him in the eye boldly at every possible chance to give him the assurance that his rude remarks had no effect upon her in the slightest. In actuality, however, they resulted in the appearance of bitter pock marks on her already porous opinion of him.

At one point, the telephone interrupted his instruction, and she let her eyes wander around the office to avoid the appearance of eavesdropping on his conversation. Her eyes settled on the picture of the girl. Ainsley soon became lost in her own thoughts, wondering who the girl was. She assumed she was Brandt's daughter because she bore such a striking resemblance to him.

"That would be my daughter," Brandt's voice broke through her thoughts as if he had been reading her mind. Her eyes automatically glanced at his left hand, where they did not find any evidence of a wedding ring. Unfortunately, Brandt noticed the glance and shifted uncomfortably in his seat.

"She's beautiful," Ainsley tried to ease the tension in the room, but Brandt answered only with an icy glare. She made a mental note that his personal life appeared to be a sore subject that should never be broached again. She was beginning to think this man consisted of only two preset temperatures: a red-hot temper and an ice-cold heart.

The rest of the day continued in quite the same manner. Brandt never let an opportunity to insult her go by, and she did her best to ignore him. He was never friendly and only smiled when he was putting her down. She enjoyed a short respite during her hour lunch break, but the afternoon proved to be more of the same.

The next two weeks followed a similar routine. She was complaining to Deedra one weekend when they were packing for the big move to the house, which Ainsley was really looking forward to. She was more than ready for a change of scenery, particularly if it meant she would be farther away from her neighbors – no more shared walls, loud music, slamming doors, or parties, not to mention the late-night love making from #12. Ainsley had been deprived of far too many good night rests, and a little peace and quiet would be more than welcome.

"Look," Deedra consoled her, "it could always be worse. At least you only have to put up with him at work. You get to come home and relax. Out of sight – out of mind, right? He's miles away being crotchety to someone else."

"Yeah, I guess you're right. At least I have a job," she replied.

The packing went quickly. Devon and some of his friends helped them load the heavier items into the moving van, and Liza's boyfriend, Jim, was supposed to meet them at the house with some of his friends to help them unload. While waiting for Jim, they unloaded all the boxes and furnishings they could carry until everything but the heavy lifting was left. Jim still hadn't shown up and wasn't answering his cell phone. The sun was going down, and they needed to return the moving truck before the rental company closed. As they debated about what to do, Deedra noticed a vehicle driving into the neighbor's garage and suggested they ask him for help.

"Besides," she said, "he looked hot from the glimpse I got of him in the driver's seat."

"Hot and probably married," Ainsley added. "Most single guys don't live in houses like this."

"C'mon, Zee! You come with me . . . please," Deedra begged, knowing very well how badly Ainsley hated having to ask strangers for help.

"Fine," Ainsley conceded. She hung back when they reached the neighbor's front door, semi-hiding behind Deedra. She was pretending to scrutinize some non-existent speck in the distant horizon when the door opened.

"Hi!" Deedra greeted the stranger a little too cheerfully. "We're your new neighbors. We wondered if we could beg a favor of you since we're in a bit of a predicament. Our moving crew never showed up to help us unload the heavy items out of the moving truck, and we wondered if you could help us lift them into the house so we can get the moving truck returned before the place closes."

"Sure, I'd be happy to help," the man said, a wave of horror sweeping over Ainsley as she recognized the voice. She reluctantly turned her gaze toward his face, her eyes involuntarily widening as they confirmed the identity of the man: Brandt Cragun. *This is not happening to me*, she thought. *He cannot be my next-door neighbor! Why is this happening to me?*

He caught sight of her at the same instant and said, "What – now you've found out where I live? You know there are laws against stalking people in this country," he spoke the words with a smirk. Between friends, his comment would have been nothing more than light banter, but their history was hardly one of friendship; therefore, Ainsley heard only another biting insult. Deedra looked at Ainsley trying to figure out if he was kidding, but seeing Ainsley's face, she surmised that something was terribly wrong.

Ainsley turned to Brandt and said coldly, "Never mind. We can manage ourselves." She grabbed Deedra by the arm and started walking across the lawn toward their house, waiting for the sound of the door slamming behind them. She was surprised, however, to find Brandt following them across the grass.

"I'm not one to go back on my word. I offered my help, and I'll help, even if it is you," he said as he climbed into the moving truck. Deedra was speechless.

"Well, I suppose desperate times call for desperate measures," Ainsley replied curtly as he directed the young women to lift one end of the sofa while he lifted the other. Liza had conveniently disappeared, apparently in search of Jim and his unreliable crew. Half an hour later, the moving truck was finally empty.

"Thanks for your help. We really appreciate it," Ainsley heard Deedra say as she busied herself in the house to avoid any more rude exchanges with Brandt.

"You're very welcome. It was my pleasure," he said transforming himself into Mr. Suave. Deedra darted back into the house as soon as he was gone.

"Zee, I must say I thought you were exaggerating when you described Mr. Road Rage, but I can see what you mean. He is a bona fide jerk to you! What are the odds of us moving next door to him – the one person in the world who seems to have a personal vendetta against you?" Ainsley shook her head in disgust.

"I'm not exactly sure what I've done to deserve this," she mumbled in response.

"There must be a reason he keeps turning up in your life. There is definitely a higher power involved in it for sure. I mean, there is no way this is a mere coincidence," Deedra speculated.

"I'm sure there is some divine reason, but I'm not so sure I want to find out what the reason is because I'm positive it involves testing me to near my breaking point," came Ainsley's dejected response.

"Why didn't you ever mention how handsome he was? Wow!" Deedra whistled.

"Seriously, Deedra, I can hardly stand to be around him, let alone look at him. If he is as handsome as you say, I will guarantee you that he is nothing more than a rotten ogre disguised as Prince Charming," Ainsley moaned. Deedra shrugged her shoulders, and they left to return the moving truck.

The next day was Sunday. Ainsley was more than a little nervous since she was transitioning to a home ward rather than a singles ward. She wasn't getting any younger after all, so she decided not to delay the inevitable. She wasn't sure how she would cope seeing women her age happily married with several children in tow, but it was something she decided to face sooner rather than later. She was surprised to see Deedra waiting for her downstairs the next morning. She had assumed Deedra would continue to attend the singles ward with Liza and Corrin.

"What are you doing?" Ainsley questioned her friend.

"Friends don't let friends go to church alone," she replied firmly.

"Oh, Deedra. You really don't have to do this for me. You know as well as I do that you'll have a much better chance of finding eligible bachelors in the singles ward," Ainsley said.

"Maybe. Maybe not. I do know that right now I'm supposed to be going to this ward with you. Don't argue with me. Just get in the car and drive," she commanded as she opened the door.

Ainsley was more than a little surprised when she received a phone call the following Saturday evening and was asked to come to church early the next morning to meet with a member of the bishopric. Surely, it was too soon for a calling. She sat down expectantly in a small room Sunday morning.

"Good morning, Sister Nelson," a man with graying hair greeted her cheerfully. "I'm Brother Whitaker, the second councilor in the bishopric. Thanks for meeting with me this morning. We're always so glad to have new members in our ward. Why don't you tell me a little bit about yourself?" Ainsley answered his questions, and then he asked, "Are you willing to serve in the ward?"

"Yes," she answered without hesitation, though her mind was screaming, *Please, not in the primary. Please, not in the primary.*

"We'd like to extend a call for you to serve in the primary," he said as her thought bubble imploded.

She suppressed her dismay and faked a smile while answering, "Of course. I'd love too," through slightly gritted teeth.

"Specifically, we'd like you to be an activity day leader for the girls ages 10 and 11. You'd meet twice a month and plan service and activities to help the girls build testimonies, strengthen families, and foster personal growth," Brother Whitaker explained as Ainsley nodded.

He continued, "Someone from the primary will contact you today to give you a more thorough orientation." He shook Ainsley's hand and sent her on her way. Ainsley knew nothing about children. In fact, she had given up babysitting for mowing lawns when she was old enough to get away from dirty diapers, snotty noses, and temper tantrums. Not that she didn't want children of her own, but she had never much liked taking care of other people's children. Now she was going to have to face one of her greatest weaknesses. She couldn't even remember what she was like as a 10-year-old, but she was overjoyed to learn after church that Deedra had been called as her co-leader.

That night a member of the primary presidency came over to orient her and Deedra. She encouraged her to give special attention to the girls who did not attend church on Sundays, reaching out to them through activity days. Ainsley felt more at ease after being oriented, until her eyes skimmed the list of girls.

There were eight girls on her list, six of whom were listed as active and two who were not. She stopped short at the name at the top of the list, starred as inactive: Bridget Cragun. She looked at the address, which confirmed that she was in fact Brandt Cragun's daughter. Ainsley could not seem to escape him. She felt as though she were in a bumper car arena, and her poor bumper car kept getting slammed into his. She couldn't seem to break free. No matter which way she turned the wheel, it led her straight back into his path.

A week later, she found herself knocking on Brandt Cragun's front door. She was more than a little nervous because she wouldn't have known that Brandt was a member of the church if Bridget's name hadn't shown up on her list. She had no idea why he didn't come to church, and she wasn't sure if he allowed his daughter to be involved in church activities. She could have telephoned, but she figured that as soon as she revealed her identity, he might hang up on her. Brandt opened the door, surprised to see her standing there.

"Is Bridget at home?" she asked.

"Bridget?" he questioned.

"Yes. I've recently been called to be the activity day leader in the Somerset Hills ward, and Bridget is on my list of girls. I wanted to deliver an invitation to Bridget for our activity this week, if you don't mind," she explained.

"That's up to Bridget not me." He stepped away from the door and called up the stairs, "Bridget, you're wanted at the door." Then, he disappeared into the kitchen. A few minutes later the girl from the picture bounded down the stairs.

"Hi, Bridget. My name is Sister Nelson, and I'm the new activity day leader in our ward. I just wanted to invite you to our first activity next week. It will be pretty convenient since I just live next door to you." Bridget took the invitation from Ainsley.

"I'd love to come," she agreed with a bright smile.

"Great! We'll see you next week then," she said as she walked down the porch. *That wasn't so bad,* she thought, *at least he was courteous enough to let me talk to his daughter without making a rude comment.* Work the next week flew by, and although Brandt's attitude didn't appear to change any, she was learning to deal with him.

Bridget came as promised to the activity, which consisted of several get-to-know-you games, so Deedra and Ainsley could learn a little bit more about the girls. They had a good turn-out with five out of the eight girls attending. Ainsley noted the different sports and activities in which each girl was involved, so she could try to attend some of their extracurricular activities as well. Jenna and Summer were both on the same gymnastics team, and Bridget knew Neela and Heather from soccer, although they didn't play on the same team. All the girls were in the same class at school, so they had a lot in common, and Bridget was at ease with the other girls.

Before the activity ended, Jenna asked, "Hey, Bridget why don't you come to church on Sundays?" Little girls didn't employ much tact, and Ainsley tensed up, hoping Jenna hadn't offended her.

"Oh, I go to church in my aunt and uncle's ward with my cousins," she answered. She didn't mention anything about her dad, so Ainsley assumed he didn't attend himself.

"Would you like to come to our ward sometime?" Ainsley jumped in.

"Sure," Bridget answered excitedly.

"How about on Sunday? I can pick you up at 8:50, if that's okay with your dad," Ainsley pressed.

"He won't care," she said nonchalantly. Thus, Ainsley had befriended Bridget Cragun, the only daughter of her nemesis. Ainsley was surprised at how readily the girls accepted her, and she found herself looking forward to seeing them not only at activity days, but at church as well. Two weeks in a row, Bridget went to church with her and sat by her and Deedra during sacrament meeting. Bridget appeared to be nothing like her father. She was friendly and gregarious and seemed to fit right in with the rest of the girls her age. Ainsley often wondered why Brandt didn't attend church, but then again, after witnessing his profane outburst two and a half months earlier, she wasn't overly surprised either. At least Bridget wasn't her father's daughter, full of anger and spite.

Ainsley noted all the changes that had occurred over the past few months with the new job, the move, and the calling. She decided that although change was difficult, in retrospect, it was a beneficial kind of difficult that made her stretch and grow in ways that she wouldn't have otherwise.

A Thief in the Night

Deedra, Liza, and Corrin had all gone to Seattle for the weekend for the wedding of Liza's sister. While Ainsley really needed to get away, she couldn't get out of work early enough on Friday. She hated being the new kid on the block at work because she felt she had to work twice as hard to prove herself – to keep her head off the chopping block if positions had to be cut in the current economic downfall. She had to make herself invaluable, and her assignment to the integration program would do just that, if she did it well. She worked long hours without extra compensation and without complaint. Once she was trained and understood how all the software and programs worked, she was sure the long hours would subside as well, but for now, she'd just have to deal with it.

The clock read 7:00 when she finally managed to pull herself away from work to go home. The place was lonely without Deedra. She ate cold cereal for dinner and plopped down in front of the TV. *Yet another exciting Friday night in the life of Ainsley Tyne Nelson,* she thought as she clicked through the stations only to find nothing of interest on. She shut the TV off and decided to check her e-mail instead. Scrolling through the 58 new e-mails in her inbox, she found nothing but junk, junk, and annoying forwards.

"Strike two," she said to herself. She looked at her calendar, surprised that May was already half over. She still hadn't planned her activity day for the following week or the semi-annual recognition night she had scheduled for the following month. She decided to read her scriptures before digging into her files and idea books. After an hour, she found her eyes involuntarily drooping due to one too many late nights over the past week, so she decided to turn in early. By the time she was finished with her nightly routine, it was already 10:30. She checked the doors for a second time and turned in for the night.

She was startled awake by a loud noise. Though her eyes were still heavy with sleep, she focused on the red blur of numbers on her alarm clock: 2:35. Her heart started to pound as she tried to reassure herself that she was just imagining things – freaking herself out because she was alone in the house. She tried to quell her fears by reassuring herself that these types of things never happened to her. They were the substance of horror movies, but she thought she better check it out just in case. She stood up.

A second loud bang, shattering glass, and the thud of footsteps coming up the stairs cemented her feet to the floor. She had nowhere to go. Her room was at the top of the stairs, so she couldn't use her bedroom door. The drop from the window was too high for her to escape that way, and there wasn't time. She had no weapon. Her heart pumped harder with each passing second, and the adrenaline coursed through her veins. She could either hide in the closet or under her bed.

She dashed under the bed, forgetting that she had started to store her food storage under it. With all the #10 cans and water, she couldn't fit. She bolted for the closet, quietly trying to shut the bi-fold door from the inside while clamoring over shoes and scrapbooking supplies to crouch in the corner. Her breathing came heavily, and she tried to calm herself down by praying, pleading for help. She heard the door open. If only she had thought of grabbing her cell phone in her panic, not that it would have done her much good. She couldn't talk while trying to hide just inches from her potential assailant whom she could see through the cracks in the doors while she kneeled amidst the shoes.

She watched the intruder shuffle through her dresser drawers and caught a glint of silver, shiny metal in his hand as the moonlight filtered through the blinds. Her heart sank at the sight of the gun. She continued to watch as the intruder began pulling the drawers out and dumping their contents everywhere, cursing under his breath. The heavy-set man was clad in black and appeared to be alone, although any accomplices could have been ransacking the main level.

He moved to the bed and knelt to look under it, throwing cans of wheat against the wall in a rage. It was only a matter of time before he came to the closet. Ainsley's mind was racing through a thousand scenarios. She had to think fast. What had she learned in her self-defense class? Go for the eyes, the groin, or the throat, but he had a gun.

She could see his dark figure coming toward the closet, and she withdrew, pressing herself against the wall. Time seemed to slow down as he opened the doors. She had to act fast since she had the element of surprise. Surely, he would search the closet as thoroughly as he had done the rest of the room. As soon as the door opened, she found that her head was level with his crotch, but she was concealed by her long dresses, so he didn't notice her. Thank heaven she didn't wear short skirts. She'd have to make a mental note of that for her activity on modesty, if she lived to tell the tale. She couldn't see the gun, but she knew she had to make a move. Having no other choice, she punched him with all the energy she could muster – the force of the blow surprising even herself as the adrenaline added to the propulsion of the movement. She heard the gun fall with a thud onto the floor.

The man let out a groan of pain and fell to his knees directly in front of her, blocking her escape. She didn't hesitate a moment, but sprang to her feet and scrambled over him, scratching and kicking as she went. He grabbed for one of her legs, but she kicked free and heel-kicked him in the head several times before untangling herself. She fled down the stairs screaming at the top of her lungs, hoping that he wouldn't shoot her in the back as she ran. She did not know what awaited her at the bottom of the stairs nor did she think about it. She just ran and screamed, praying that someone in the neighborhood would wake up. She was surprised to find the front door open and crossed its threshold in two giant leaps.

Out of the darkness on the porch, she saw the shadow of a figure, and she caught the gleam of an aluminum baseball bat as the streetlight showed down upon it. She was frozen with fear as the figure approached her, pushing her forcefully out of the door's entryway.

"Where is he?" She recognized Brandt's voice immediately. He must have heard her screaming or heard all the glass breaking.

"Upstairs," she croaked with a hoarse voice.

"Go wait on my porch. The police should be here any minute," he directed in a whisper.

"But he has a gun," she managed to say as she inched toward the Cragun house.

"Just go," he commanded. Several lights were on in the neighboring houses, and Ainsley could see worried faces peeking out to see what all the commotion was about. Just then, a police siren sounded, which was shortly followed by the

29

sight of flashing red and blue lights rounding the corner. Brandt stepped away from her porch, slowly lowering his bat and walking toward the sidewalk, careful not to turn his back toward her front door. The policeman jumped out of his patrol car with his weapon drawn, and Brandt called out to him that the intruder was upstairs and possibly armed.

A second squad car came screeching to a stop. Both officers entered the house. Moments later they emerged, dragging the maimed criminal to the nearest car. An officer spoke to Brandt for a few minutes while Ainsley sat paralyzed on his front steps, watching as though seeing a clip from someone else's bizarre life. An officer approached her.

"Miss?" he asked. "Are you okay?"

"I . . . I . . . thinks s-so," she muttered, hugging her arms tightly around herself. "I . . . I'm just a little sh . . . shaken," she stammered in a voice that sounded foreign in her own ears.

"I'm going to need you to tell me what happened," he prompted. Ainsley nodded her head numbly and proceeded to describe as best she could the events that had unfolded just moments before. At the time, everything happened so fast, and yet the images were replaying in her head in slow motion. An eerie feeling crept over her as she finished recounting the last vivid memory, and her body began to shake involuntarily, not from the cold of the early morning, but from the sudden realization of the reality of her ordeal.

"Is there someone I can call for you or somewhere you can go?" the officer asked, concerned.

"Um . . . no . . . I'll be fine," she said unconvincingly. She was terrified to go back into that house alone tonight, but she had nowhere else to go. Her parents were hours away. Her friends wouldn't get back until early afternoon even if she did call them. She didn't know anyone in the ward well enough to call at 3:00 in the morning or whatever time it was. She realized she had no idea how much time had lapsed since she had last looked at her alarm clock. The officer rejoined Brandt and the second policeman, and they continued their conference, apparently comparing the different accounts of the break-in.

Ainsley wandered back to her front porch and sat down on the steps as though in a daze. She suddenly felt exhausted, too tired to even cry, and she couldn't stop shaking. She watched the police cars drive away. She watched the lights go out in the neighbors' windows. She watched Brandt retreat into the shadows. All was quiet. All was dark except the lights in her own house, which the policemen had left on after they finished processing the crime scene. The front door was wide open, and her sense of security was as broken as the front window through which the intruder had entered. *Of all the houses on this block, why mine?* Ainsley questioned silently when a voice startled her from her thoughts.

"Are you all right?" She looked up to make sure it was Brandt – his voice sounded different without the disdain and sarcasm. Her eyes shifted back down to her bare feet, which throbbed from kicking her assailant so fiercely. She couldn't answer. Her energy was spent. As he sat down beside her, he put his arm around her, drawing her toward him as her animosity toward him slowly began to retreat. Wrapped in his safe embrace, she laid her head against his chest. The rhythmic beating of his heart lulled her to sleep.

She awoke with a start and found herself on a black leather sofa, snuggled up in a furry pink blanket. Her head felt like it might explode, and her eyes were slits against the puffiness of their perimeters. *Where am I?* she thought. The memories of last night came scampering back to her mind like an unwanted rodent wandering in a once silent hall. The last thing she remembered was sitting on her porch with Brandt's arm around her, and then nothing. Her mind was blank. He must have carried her to his house and put her to sleep on his couch.

The house appeared to be empty. Either Brandt was still sleeping, or he was gone, and so was Bridget.

She folded the blanket, leaving it on the couch, and snuck out the front door. She walked the few steps to her own front door, surprised to find it closed and the glass from the broken window cleaned up. The window even had a large piece of cardboard taped to it, where the glass should have been. She turned the knob to go in the house and found it unlocked. She wasn't sure if she was prepared to see the damage the intruder had done.

Taking a deep breath, she stepped inside. To her surprise, she found everything to be in perfect order. She looked up the stairs, not sure if she was ready to deal with what awaited her there, but the sight of the sun streaming through the house instead of the blackness of night washed away most of her fear. She could do this. She was a strong, independent woman, not a frightened child who needed to be coddled.

When she reached her bedroom door, she found everything cleaned up and put away. There were some dents in the wall from the impact of the wheat cans and what appeared to be some blood stains that someone had tried to clean up on the floor by the closet. She must have hit the man harder than she thought. Her eyes settled on her alarm clock: 4:00. That couldn't be right, could it? Had she been asleep all day? She wondered if Brandt had cleaned her house while she slept. Such compassionate behavior would certainly have been contrary for the Brandt she knew, but he had also shown another surprising side of himself by comforting her last night.

She decided to shower and change out of her pajamas, which were an awful reminder of last night. Once she was cleaned up, she called her parents to tell them what had happened. Of course, her mom went into hysterics, reminding Ainsley that she had warned her not to move into that house in the first place.

An hour later, her mom was calm enough to hang up the phone. Not two seconds after she hung up, the phone rang again.

"Hello?" Ainsley answered warily, not recognizing the number that flashed on the screen.

"Hello, Ainsley. This is Sister Murphy, the Relief Society President," she introduced herself.

"Oh, yes, hello."

"I heard what happened last night and just wondered if there was anything else we could do for you," she said.

Anything else? Ainsley repeated in her head. The Relief Society must have come over to clean the house. She felt a surge of relief knowing that a woman had put her personal items back in her dresser instead of Brandt.

"Brother Cragun called this morning to let me know and asked if I could bring some ladies over to straighten your room up before you got home. He'd already taken care of the rest," she explained. Ainsley could hardly believe what she was hearing! Brandt had called the Relief Society President? Had he cleaned up everything else himself?

"I can't tell you how grateful I am to you for coming over. I don't know if I would have been able to deal with seeing everything like it was last night, again. I really can't thank you enough," Ainsley said, her voice cracking as her eyes teared up unexpectedly.

"You're very welcome," she said, "but, how are you doing? Is there anything at all you need?"

"I'm fine, really. You've already done too much," Ainsley reassured her several times that all was well before Sister Murphy would hang up the phone. Ainsley decided not to call Deedra. There was no need to rush Liza's visit home. Besides keeping Ainsley company, there was nothing they could do now. They would be home by Sunday evening anyway, so she would just have to make it through one more night. She noticed the sun was starting to sink behind the hills, and her courage sank with it, fear creeping back with each lengthening shadow. She turned all the lights on in the house, grabbed a kitchen knife, and turned her music up as loud as she dared. This was going to be a long night.

Her stomach growled as she realized she hadn't eaten all day. She went to the kitchen to see what she could scrounge up. She was supposed to go grocery shopping today, but that had completely slipped her mind. She was leaning into the pantry when she heard someone call, "Hey!" through the cardboard posing as a window. She released a blood curdling scream and reached for the kitchen knife on the counter, only to see Brandt's face peeking through the side of the window that hadn't been broken. *Oh, how many times I've wanted to hurt him for all his insults and rudeness. Here's my chance,* she thought sarcastically. Then, she remembered last night and everything he had done to help her today. She turned her music down as she left the kitchen to unlock the front door, knife still in hand.

"I don't think you'll be needing that knife. You do a pretty good job in hand-to-hand combat," he laughed.

"What are you talking about?" she queried, her brow knit with confusion.

"Didn't they tell you? You broke that guy's nose and fractured his jaw, not to mention the fact that he'll probably never father children," he explained with another chuckle.

"I did?"

"Yeah, you did. So why don't you put the knife down?"

Ainsley motioned for him to come inside as she returned the knife to its chopping block in the kitchen, her hand still trembling from the fright. She took a deep breath to calm herself before returning to the living room.

34

"So, what's with the music and all the lights? Warding off any repeat offenders?" he asked.

"Yeah, I guess you could say that," Ainsley's face turned red as she spoke. "About last night. . ."

"Oh, I hope you aren't upset that I took you to my house," he apologetically interrupted. "I didn't know what else to do. I couldn't just leave you here, and I didn't want to wake you up."

"Uh . . . no . . . no. I just wanted to thank you, that's all. I mean for all your help. I'm glad you decided to help a damsel in distress instead of just peeking out your window like everyone else did," she clarified.

"Oh, is that what I was doing? Rescuing a damsel in distress?" He folded his arms as he spoke and puffed out his chest, apparently imitating a knight in shining armor.

"I . . . I didn't mean it like that. Oh . . . never mind. I suppose next you're going to accuse me of hiring the intruder in a scheme to weasel into your house or something equally unlikely and obnoxious, or maybe you hired him in a last-ditch effort to rid yourself of your supposed disaster magnet and felt a little guilty at my likely demise, so you sauntered over repentantly to redeem yourself," she retorted, remembering her first encounter with the ever-endearing Mr. Road Rage.

"I guess I deserve that," came his unexpected response. "So . . ."

"So . . ." she repeated, the awkwardness hung in the air like a bird waiting to release its white vengeance on its next unsuspecting victim.

"So, I was headed to grab some fast food and wondered if maybe. . .you'd. . . like to come. . . with me," Brandt actually stammered. Ainsley didn't answer. This was so unlike Brandt – so unexpected.

"Are you okay?" she asked sarcastically. "Are you sure you didn't hit your head last night in all the excitement and confusion, or maybe you've hooked up some candid camera somewhere so you can have a big laugh at me later?"

"Sorry for offering," he shook his head and turned to leave. Ainsley realized that he was serious. This wasn't some joke. She reached out and grabbed his arm to stop his retreat.

"Wait," she said, realizing that she really did need some company, even if it was Brandt. She didn't want to be alone in the house at night. When he turned around, she noticed for the first time the void in his eyes begin to fill with liquid chocolate. Something had obviously changed his attitude toward her, or was it her attitude toward him?

"I'm starving. I haven't eaten all day, and I was supposed to go grocery shopping today," she said quickly. Noticing that she was still holding onto his arm, she let go, embarrassed. She turned away so he wouldn't see her fuchsia face. Brandt didn't seem to notice her discomfiture.

"Do you want me to drive?" she asked with a smile.

"Not a chance," he said as he walked out the door. She followed him to his Honda, and he opened the door for her. She felt stupid. What was she doing with him of all people – the one person who made her feel small and insignificant whenever he could? She looked in the backseat half expecting to see Bridget smiling back at her, but it was empty.

"Where's Bridget?" she asked.

"She's at a slumber party with her cousins," he replied. Ainsley looked disappointed. She was hoping to take Bridget to church with her again.

"Don't worry," he assured her. "She's going to church with my brother Brady and his family." Ainsley didn't reply as she stared out the window. The fast-food place wasn't that far away, but she wondered why he chose to go through the drive-thru instead of just eating inside. He handed her the bag and the drinks and drove back to his house. Ainsley couldn't help but be suspicious of him. She felt like he was a bear, mercilessly toying with his next meal before going in for the kill. However, she followed him into his house and sat down at the table.

"So, why the sudden change of heart?" she asked yielding to her curiosity between bites of her hamburger.

"What do you mean?" he asked innocently.

"As if you don't know," she prodded.

"Know what?"

"C'mon. Don't play dumb with me. You have hated me since the first day you laid eyes on me, and you go out of your way to insult me whenever you can," he tried to interrupt, but she went on. "Oh, I've kept this bottled up for far too long, and I'm finally going to get it out in the open. I think you must be into some serious voodoo or something because ever since I met you, bad things keep happening to me. What are you? Some kind of assassin sent to murder my future – to drive me to the brink of insanity to see if I'll break? Or are you some devil sent to torment me – whose very appearance brings catastrophe into my life? I've never been in a car accident IN MY LIFE until you came along. What did you do? Park directly behind me so I'd hit you? I've never worn mismatched shoes to a job interview and never been burglarized. I've never been belittled or publicly humiliated by anyone until you came into my life. And no one has ever told me to go to H – E – double hockey sticks before! So, what is your deal?" she demanded, expecting to see the dark void return to his eyes, but it did not. They remained as soft and expressive as before with no hint of retaliation darkening any part of them.

"First of all, bravo! I didn't know how much more you could take without blowing up. Secondly, all your assertions are wrong. I don't have anything against you personally," he answered nonchalantly.

"Oh, do you treat all of your acquaintances like that?"

"Only those I like," her French fry stuck in her throat when he spoke, and she started to choke. When she finally stopped coughing, she managed to mutter, "You've GOT to be kidding me! Is that all you have to say for yourself?"

"Look. There's no excuse for how I've been treating you, and I apologize. That's not good enough, I know. An apology can't make up for the last few months."

"You can say that again!"

"Will you stop interrupting so I can talk? The first time we met, I was having a very bad day, and I took it out on you. My ex-wife had promised my daughter she would take her for the weekend, and she had just called to blow her off. Bridget hasn't seen her in more than two years. Then, she had the audacity to tell me she was getting married and asked me if I would tell Bridget she was getting a new dad. I only reacted to you how I wished I had reacted to her. I felt terrible about it when I got to work, but I figured I'd never see you again, so what would it matter, right?" He stopped to take a drink.

"I could forgive you for that, but what about everything else – all the rude comments at work?" she pressed.

"Honestly, I was just joking around with you, but you took it the wrong way. I didn't bother enlightening you. I've never seen anyone roll their eyes as discreetly as you do when you're annoyed."

"How was I supposed to know you were just teasing me? You never even cracked a smile," she said. "By the way, that's a really lame explanation for practically ruining my life, and it still doesn't explain why everything goes wrong when you're around."

"I guess that's a matter of perspective. Number one: the accident – nobody got hurt, at least physically anyway. Number two: You got the job, even though you backed into a member of the interview committee just hours before. Number three: You're still alive and you fought off a burglar. There are some bragging rights attached to that. So, I'd call them blessings in disguise."

"You've got a valid argument there, I guess," she reluctantly admitted.

"I really am sorry for taking my frustrations out on you when we first met and for giving you a rough time at work. I was embarrassed about the way I treated you after the accident. Continuing the ruse was easier than apologizing at the time. I keep people at arm's length and being a complete jerk tends to accomplish that. I hope you can accept my apology, however lame it may be, so we can be friends," he reached out to shake her hand across the table.

"I appreciate the apology, and I will work on forgiving you," she conceded as she shook his hand. The food was gone, and he cleared up the garbage.

"By the way," Ainsley asked, "how did you get to my house so fast?"

"For some reason I couldn't sleep. I tossed and turned for a couple of hours, but I couldn't seem to shake this feeling that I needed to get up. I finally went downstairs to check everything out only to find that nothing seemed amiss. I was wide awake by then, so I picked up a book to read. Before I got through the first page, I thought I heard breaking glass. When I peeked out the window to investigate, I saw a shadow moving in the bushes by your living room window. I called 911. When I got off the phone, I decided to go over, just in case. I grabbed my baseball bat and had just crossed your lawn when I heard a scream. Then, you came flying down the stairs."

"Lucky for me you couldn't sleep," she said, although she knew very well that luck had very little to do with it, but this was neither the time nor the place to give Brandt a discourse on the workings of the Holy Ghost.

"Listen," Brandt said, "you're more than welcome to sleep on the couch again." The offer was tempting.

"Ah, but what would the neighbors say seeing me slip quietly away from your house two days in a row. That's much too scandalous for a man with an impressionable young daughter."

"It's your call. I don't really care what they think."

"Thanks, but I'll pass," she dismissed his offer, grabbing her purse from the coat rack. "By the way, thanks for cleaning the place up for me. I really appreciate it." He just smiled as he closed the door behind her.

The lights were still ablaze inside her house when she opened the door. She sat on the couch, but every noise made her jump. Looking at the stairs made her shudder. There was no way she could stay there alone. She rummaged around downstairs for a blanket and ran back to Brandt's house as though someone was in hot pursuit. Her hand knocked nervously on the door, and she heard the TV click off, followed by heavy footsteps crossing the hardwood floors to the door. The porch light flickered to life as the door opened slightly, and she was relieved to see Brandt's face looking at her curiously. A half smile crossed his lips, and she noticed a deep dimple in his left cheek.

"Change of plans?" he asked, eyeing the blanket in her arms as he opened the door to let her in. He had changed into an old white T-shirt and black basketball shorts.

"I couldn't quite make it to the Emerald City to ask for my courage," she mocked herself.

"I was just turning in for the night, so feel free to take the couch," he offered as he shut and locked the door. "And there's no need to worry. I've got an alarm system installed, so there will be lots of warning if anyone tries to hit the neighborhood again."

"Oh, I'm not worried. I came prepared," she said, holding Deedra's travel sized can of pepper spray in her hand, which she found in the front closet with the blanket. Brandt rolled his eyes.

"Looks like I better sleep with my goggles on tonight, just in case you sleepwalk," he joked. "Goodnight, Ainsley." For some reason, she was surprised to hear him call her by name because he never had before. He tossed her the pillow she had slept on the night before, which he had left out just in case.

"My friends call me Zee," she said instinctively.

"Okay, then. Goodnight, Zee."

"Goodnight yourself, and thank you," she said as she unfolded her blanket. He ascended the stairs without saying another word.

About an hour later, Brandt realized that he had forgotten to arm the alarm system, so he crept downstairs, hoping not to disturb Ainsley. He walked silently past the couch to the keypad on the wall by the front door. After arming the system, he pressed a sticky note to the alarm pad with the disarming code, knowing that Ainsley would most likely want to sneak off early the next morning.

As he walked by the couch again to go upstairs, he saw Ainsley sleeping peacefully. Her long hair had fallen over her face, and her mouth was slightly ajar. He watched for a moment, overcome by a sudden yearning to hold her in his arms as he did the night before – to feel another heart beat beside his again – to hear her breathing near his ear as she slept – to feel the touch of her soft skin against his own – to smell the faint but lingering aroma of her perfume. He wanted to reach out and brush the hair out of her face and trace his finger along the soft lines of her jaw. He wanted to press his lips against hers, tasting love and life again. He wanted to, but he didn't. He also wanted to erase the cruelty she had endured from him, expelling it from her mind. He wanted her to see him not as the monster he masqueraded as for the sake of his pride, but as the man he had once been.

For the past three years, ever since Malissa's unexpected departure from his life, he had erected a fortress. He had become a stone sentinel forcing himself to guard his fractured soul, ready to defend at the first sign of a breach in the wall. He allowed only his daughter the liberty of passage into his heart for they shared the same pain – the same knife had slashed both their hearts asunder. He had gathered the broken pieces and sewn them back together as best he could, though the stitches were uneven and loose.

He had prayed like never before, begging for the healing balm of Gilead to cure the rest. Yet, he also buried a part of himself deep inside, hoping to suffocate it from existence, so he would never feel that searing pain again. Now, he felt those buried feelings tunneling to the surface, desperate for a breath of fresh air to renew their fragile life – pleading for a second chance. The person who could rescue him was right in front of him, digging him out without even knowing what she was doing. He tucked his yearnings back inside and walked up the stairs, retreating from a war he was not yet ready to wage.

Sure enough, Ainsley heard her cell phone alarm go off at 5:30 am, prematurely dragging her from a restful sleep. Because the sun was up to chase away the shadows and silence the strange sounds amplified by the night into frequencies of fear, she knew she could return home. She smiled at Brandt's sticky note as she quickly disabled the alarm system. Locking the door behind her, she trudged back into her own disturbed sanctuary.

A few hours later, she found herself sitting alone in sacrament meeting. No Bridget. No Deedra. Just herself, alone. Her mind zoomed forward fifty years, and she imagined herself sitting in the same spot, still alone. Was that what the future held for her – loneliness? Not wanting to pursue that train of thought, she tuned back into the speaker who was talking about forgiveness. A slow smile spread across her face. At least she had made peace with her arch enemy. That was something to be happy about. Hopefully, life at work would be a little easier for her now, not having to dance on eggshells around Brandt or employing evasive maneuvers to avoid him. She found it rather difficult to dodge the one person to whom she had to talk to get her job done. Maybe the burglary was an answer to her fervent prayers about softening Brandt Cragun's heart toward her so she could at least endure the days spent with him with less difficulty. Her prayer certainly was answered in a very unexpected way in the form of a thief in the night!

Turning the Tide

The following weekend, Ainsley found herself at a youth soccer game to support three of her activity day girls who were participating in the spring soccer season. From the bleachers, Ainsley spotted Bridget and decided to wish her good luck before the game began. She had already spoken to Neela and Heather, who were on the opposing team. As Bridget and Ainsley were talking, Bridget's eyes brightened when she noticed the approach of two people with four children running rampant around them. Bridget grabbed Ainsley's hand, yanking her toward them.

"Hey, this is Zee. I mean Ainsley," she announced. Ainsley had dropped the formality of using Sister Nelson with her activity girls, and they took to calling her Zee because that's what Deedra called her. Ainsley was speechless as she stared at the man's face because she was staring at Brandt, yet she knew it couldn't be Brandt.

"From the look on your face, Bridget never mentioned her Uncle Brady was her dad's twin brother," he laughed.

"No, she didn't," she admitted. Just then, Brandt approached from behind.

"Hey, sweetheart," he said to Bridget, kissing her on the forehead. Then, turning to Ainsley, he said, "I see you've met my look alike."

"Yes, but I won't hold that against him," she jabbed, rousing laughter from Brady and his wife.

"Well, it's nice to finally meet you," said Brady, holding out his hand. As she shook it, he added, "We've heard a lot about you." He gave Brandt a not-so-subtle smile, which Brandt returned with a glare. A whistle blew, signaling the game's beginning, and Bridget raced off to join her teammates.

As the Cragun's moved toward the bleachers, Brady's wife turned toward her, "You're welcome to sit by us if you don't mind some loud cheering and four rowdy kids crawling around you."

"I'd hate to impose," Ainsley protested.

"Nonsense," she said. "Besides, I could use some female company for a change." She motioned toward the four boys wrestling their way to the bleachers. "I also have twin girls who are 10, but they're at a birthday party today," she explained, and then added, "I'm Eve, by the way."

"Nice to meet you, Eve," Ainsley said.

"Well, how about it?" she asked again. Ainsley looked at the full bleachers, noticing that the seat she had been sitting in was now occupied, and nodded in acceptance.

"Why not?" she shrugged and tagged along behind the Cragun boys with Eve at her side.

"So, you know Bridget from activity girls I gather?"

"Yes, and I'm also her next-door neighbor. She told me she'd been going to church with you. I hope you didn't mind her coming with me."

"Not at all. It's been good for her to get to know the girls she goes to school with. We've told Brandt he needs to start going to his own ward, but I guess he's too comfortable going with us to make the transition." Confusion crossed Ainsley's face. Eve detected it and guessed, "You thought Brandt was inactive, didn't you?"

"I guess I assumed so, though the subject never came up. Bridget never mentioned him going to church with you when I offered to take her to our ward."

"Brandt lived with us for a month or so when he first moved here. Then, he rented a little duplex in our ward for about two and a half years before the owner sold it. He just bought his house a few months ago, but he's been dragging his feet about transferring wards. He loved his calling in the young men's program, but the bishop finally gave him the boot on Sunday. He was released and strongly urged to start attending his own ward. So, I'm sure you'll be relieved of your little charge this Sunday," she elaborated.

"It was no trouble. In fact, I looked forward to it." Ainsley was still trying to process the fact that she had misjudged Brandt so badly, not that she should have been judging him at all. She was not enjoying the rancid taste of humble pie. They reached the bleachers and sat down to watch Bridget, while she also cheered for Neela and Heather. The game was over before she knew it. Surprisingly, she had felt very comfortable around Brady and Eve, and she was glad she had joined them.

"You know, we're having a little barbecue at our house tonight. We'd love it if you came," Eve offered. Ainsley looked uncomfortably at Brandt, but he was busy kicking a soccer ball with Bridget.

Brady noticed her hesitation and the direction of her glance and called out,

"Hey Brandt, why don't you convince your neighbor here to join us at our barbecue?"

Brandt's head snapped up in disbelief, but he didn't have a chance to respond because Bridget came bounding up to Ainsley, pleading, "Oh, please come. Then, you can meet Teagan and Traci." Ainsley felt like she was backed into a corner with no way of excusing herself from the invitation.

"All right, if you're sure you want a complete stranger crashing your family party," she stated.

"Brandt," Brady said, "why don't you give her a ride, so we don't crowd my cul-de-sac with cars?" Now Brandt was backed into a corner, and Ainsley couldn't tell whether he was madder at Brady for pushing him there or at Eve for inviting Ainsley in the first place.

"That's fine," he said, glowering at Brady, but his expression softened as he turned to Ainsley and said, "Why don't you come over around 5:00? That should give Bridget plenty of time to get showered and ready to go."

"Okay," Ainsley answered, still trying to find a way to weasel out of the invitation.

When 5:00 rolled around, Ainsley was fully prepared to go over to Brandt's house and back out of the whole deal with the lame excuse that something had come up last minute. She knocked on the door, and he invited her in.

"Bridget's not quite ready yet, so you can have a seat." He sat down in a recliner as she settled down on the couch that she had used for a bed exactly one week ago.

"Actually, I just came over to say that something came up, and I won't be able to go," she said.

"No, you didn't. That's just an excuse because you think I don't want you to come, which isn't true either. Bridget is really looking forward to having you there. For some reason, she's grown quite attached to you in the short time she's known you."

"I do tend to have that effect on people," she interrupted. "Present company excluded of course." He gave her his little half smile.

"So, you'll still come then, in spite of me?" he asked.

"No, I'll come if you leave your spite at home," she retorted.

"It's a deal," he agreed.

"You might have said that you were attending church with Bridget instead of leaving me to assume that you were inactive," she chided.

"You never asked, but I can see that Eve has enlightened you today."

"Who would ask a question like that to someone they hardly know? I mean, I did think it was a little odd that you called Sister Murphy to help clean up my room after the burglary. But Bridget never mentioned that you went to church with her, and I didn't want to pry. Then, you let her come to church alone with me, without even offering to take her yourself. Isn't that a little hokey?" she asked.

"Bridget probably assumed that everyone already knew her dad went to church with her. She knew that I was going to change wards at the end of the month anyway, and she was thrilled that you asked her to come with you. She didn't want me tagging along," he explained.

"So, what was up with all the swearing when we first met then? I would have never guessed you were even a member based on our first encounter," she said. He looked away, embarrassed by the reminder of his behavior that day.

"That's a teenage vice I'm still struggling to overcome. Unfortunately, when I get angry it creeps back out sometimes," he rationalized. "Remember, I've already apologized for that. It wasn't one of my better days." Just then, Bridget came down the stairs, and Brandt said under his breath, "Ah, saved by the

Bridge."

"Let's go," she said, heading for the front door with Ainsley and Brandt close behind. It was 5:30 by the time they arrived at Brady's house. The family was already in the backyard dishing up their plates.

"So, where's your salad, Ainsley?" Brady asked.

"Oh, I didn't even think…" she started, but Brandt interrupted, "It's better just to ignore him." Brady began to laugh as he escorted Ainsley to the plates.

"Glad you could grace us with your presence, my lady," he said with a little bow.

Eve punched him in the arm as she remarked, "Leave the guest alone, and help Kellan with his hot dog."

"At your command," he saluted his wife and turned to help his youngest son cut his hot dog. Bridget introduced Ainsley to the twins, Teagan and Traci, who almost looked identical to Bridget. Then, she was introduced to the four brothers: Thane was 8, Rylan was 6, Holden was 4, and Kellan was 2. Dinner was lively with the seven children dancing about instead of eating, but the real fun came after dinner when Thane suggested they play Boochie. Ainsley had never heard of the game before, so they explained the rules.

"First you toss the foam Boochie target," Holden said.

"Then you try to land your colored bean ball and ring as close to the target as possible," Thane instructed. "Whoever comes closest gets 2 points, and the next closest gets 1 point."

"Oh, so it's like Bocce?" Ainsley said.

"Bocce ball with a twist," Traci corrected.

"You keep track of your score on this wrist tracker, which also tells you how you have to throw the ball each round," Bridget explained.

"The more points you get, the harder the challenge. The first team to 11 wins," Teagan chimed in.

"I'm on Uncle Brandt's team," Holden called out, and so the teams were split up: Traci and Eve, along with Kellan, Brandt and Holden, Bridget and Ainsley, Thane and Teagan, and Brady and Rylan. The game only included enough pieces for four teams, so Brady found another ball and ring for his team. Ainsley had so much fun playing the game, she nearly forgot she wasn't part of the family. Everyone laughed when Rylan tried to throw the ball underneath one leg, and when Eve had to roll the ball off her head.

Ainsley was utterly confused when her wrist scorer told her she had to serve and slap her hoop, but somehow, she managed, while making an utter fool of herself. On the verge of winning, Brandt had to put his forehead on the ground while he tried to throw his ball, which would have been awkward enough if Kellan hadn't climbed onto his back as well. He had barely thrown his ball when all the children dog-piled him. Ainsley laughed until her side hurt, and then it was time for s'mores. Too soon, the evening was over. She thanked Brady and Eve, and the trio headed home. Bridget was asleep before they pulled into the driveway.

"Thanks," Ainsley said as she opened the front door, so Brandt could carry Bridget upstairs.

"No," he answered, "thank you." She let herself out the front door and walked home, feeling happier than she had in a long time. She found herself glancing out the tall window upstairs to catch a glimpse of Brandt since the window showed into his hallway. She would have only been able to see the tip of his head at the very most, but that would have been enough.

The next day at church, Brandt showed up with Bridget. Bridget took her place by Ainsley, leaving Brandt no choice but to sit in their row as well. Since Bridget already knew where Primary was, Brandt didn't have an excuse to exit the chapel, which was also where Sunday school was held. Knowing no one else in the ward, he remained seated by Ainsley. When Sunday school started, the teacher asked Ainsley to introduce her guest. Her face went bright red as she searched for the right words.

"Oh, I'll introduce myself. I'm Brandt Cragun. My daughter and I have just moved into the ward, next door to Sister Nelson, in fact." The teacher welcomed him as everyone continued to stare in their direction. Deedra chuckled under her breath, and Ainsley elbowed her into silence.

That afternoon, Ainsley wandered into the backyard. She looked at Corrin's flowers, which were wilting from lack of water. She hooked up the hose, but when she turned it on, water shot out, dousing her. She screeched as the cold water saturated her clothes.

"Everything okay over there?" she heard Brandt call from his backyard. She hadn't noticed him.

"Yeah. I'm just having a problem with my hose," she hollered back. She went to the fence that bordered Brandt's house, dragging the hose along with her.

"Hey, do you think you could take a look at this for me really quick?" she asked, pressing the nozzle near one of the openings in the slats of the fence.

"Sure, what seems to be the problem?" he asked as he approached the fence.

"Well, you see, whenever I press the lever on the nozzle, it goes like this," she pressed the nozzle, drenching him with water.

"Why you little. . ." he started to say, but she was laughing so hard she couldn't hear him. The next thing she knew, he was showering water down on her with his hose.

She fired back and after a few minutes, she said, "Okay, okay. Truce! I promise I won't spray anymore if you don't." She peeked through the fence to see Brandt dripping wet from head to toe, his hair curling more with the added moisture.

He looked as if he were in serious contemplation, and then said, "Okay, truce," while tossing his hose aside. She couldn't help herself. She aimed the nozzle right at his face, pressed the lever to deliver a direct hit, and then dropped her hose and ran screeching into her house before he could retaliate, while screaming, "My fingers were crossed!"

Monday morning arrived, and Ainsley found herself looking forward to work. She also found that she was more observant about her neighbor's comings and goings. Life was much better now that they were friends, but there was a feeling that kept trying to nudge its way into her heart – a feeling that suggested she might not be satisfied with a mere friendship with the mysterious man who kept reappearing at just the right moments.

A couple of weeks later, Ainsley decided to catch up on her scrapbooking. She was sitting on the living room floor with her supplies scattered around her when she was interrupted by a knock at the door.

"Hi, Bridget," Ainsley greeted her.

"Hey, my dad went ministering with Brother Miller. Do you mind if I hang out with you for a while?" she asked, already making herself at home on the sofa.

"Not at all. Sorry it's a bit of a mess."

"What are you working on?" she asked, eyeing the stacks of paper and pictures.

"Oh, just trying to catch up in my scrapbook," she said sitting down cross-legged in front of her mess. "Too often people just assume that the only women who enjoy scrapbooking and card-making are married women with children."

"What are you scrapbooking then?"

"All my good times and memories. Look. Here's the trip Deedra and I took to the coast a while back," she said, handing a bunch of photos to Bridget.

"What's this picture of?" she asked, turning a photo toward Ainsley.

"Oh," Ainsley said laughing at the recollection, "I buried Deedra in the sand so only her head was poking out, although all you could see from that angle was a pile of black frizzy hair." She handed the picture back to Bridget and started sifting through another stack.

"And here are some of activity days. I wouldn't want to forget about you girls, would I?" Bridget laughed at the picture that showed all of them pulling silly faces at their first activity.

"I wish I could scrapbook," she said forlornly.

"Why can't you?"

"I wouldn't know how to start or what to do. My mom wasn't into that kind of stuff, and even if she was, she's not around anymore to teach me," Bridget explained.

"I'll tell you what. You bring over your pictures sometime, and I'll help you get started. You can use my stuff. I clearly have more than enough to go around. Besides, I could use the company. Deedra's not much into this sort of stuff either. And I can show you how to make cards too," Ainsley suggested.

"Really?" Bridget said, excitement flashing across her bright little eyes.

"You bet!" Ainsley assured her.

"Do you think you could help me make something special for my dad for his birthday?" she asked.

"Sure, did you have anything in mind?" Ainsley asked.

"What about making a scrapbook for him?" she proposed.

"That's a great idea, but you'll have to be in charge of getting the pictures you want to put in it. When is his birthday, by the way?"

"Oh, it's not until October – plenty of time." she said, nestling back into the sofa with a pile of pictures and a great big smile on her face. Ainsley couldn't help but love that little girl. She looked forward to her unannounced visits, which were occurring more and more frequently lately. Most of the time her father didn't even know she'd snuck away, but he looked at Ainsley's house first because inevitably she was always there.

The following Saturday, Ainsley was standing in her driveway staring at a pathetic pile of metal. Deedra had purchased the old push lawnmower from an ad that had been in an online community marketplace, and it wasn't worthy of the title 'piece of junk,' let alone lawnmower. Ainsley had volunteered for yard duty, but the lawnmower wasn't cooperating. She couldn't get it started, try as she might. She kept pulling on the cord, adjusting the levers, and priming it, but she was having no luck, and her patience was waning. She decided to give it one more try. She turned up the volume on her music just in case the machine roared to life.

She pulled back with all her might, the cord snapping from the ancient machine, sending Ainsley hurtling through the air. She was stopped short when she hit something solid, knocked it over, and tumbled to the ground on top of it. When she opened her eyes to see what she had fallen on, she found herself lying prostrate on top of an astonished Brandt. Their eyes locked for a long moment before she saw a smile creep across his face. Still lost in his eyes, she managed to break herself free to stand up as he jumped off the ground. The moment fizzled, but there had been a moment.

"Sorry about that," she said laughing, as she pulled her ear buds out of her ears. "I didn't hear you sneak up behind me."

"I doubt you could hear much with that noise blasting like it is," he said motioning toward her phone. "I just got back from taking Bridget to swimming lessons and noticed you were having some trouble. I thought I'd offer my assistance, but it looks like you're beyond help now," he nodded in the direction of the length of cord that was still dangling from her clutched fist.

"I guess I don't know my own strength," she said. Ainsley walked over to the lawnmower and gave it a little kick. "I doubt if this tin can is coming back from the grave this time," she complained.

"I'll tell you what, I'll mow your lawn when I mow mine," he offered.

"How about I mow yours *and* mine with your mower?" she counter offered.

"I don't know about that considering what you just did to yours," he laughed.

"Oh, give me a break. That bucket of junk was on its last leg when Deedra bought it. We're lucky it has lasted as long as it has, which isn't long considering we've only had it for a month now," she said. "Yours is bound to be in better condition."

"Why are you so insistent on mowing the lawn?" he inquired. "Most people would jump at the chance to get out of that job."

"Most people haven't been cooped up in an apartment for the last nine years either. Besides, it brings back fond childhood memories. Being an only child, the yard work was the one summer chore that supported my slush puppy habit, and you can't beat the smell of fresh cut grass on a hot summer day, not to mention the green shoes. I haven't had a pair of those in a while," she explained.

"Gee, I didn't know it meant that much to you. I suppose I could relinquish my duty just this once so you can frolic in your childhood memories," he said, shaking his head. He disappeared into his house and came back out of his garage a few minutes later, pushing a brand new, bright green lawnmower.

"She's all yours," he said and went back into his house. As Ainsley mowed the lawn, her mind replayed the scene that had transpired only moments ago over and over again. She acknowledged for the first time that she really did care for Brandt as more than just a friend. She was noticing everything about him these days, from the comments she made that inspired his dimple to reveal itself to the way he knit his eyebrows when Bridget made a corny or off-the-wall comment. She waited to hear his voice greet her at work, and she was constantly glancing out her windows to catch a glimpse of him. Her heart raced when she heard his SUV pull into his driveway, and she anticipated the doorbell when he came to get Bridget after she had come over for one of her unexpected visits.

She tried to clear her mind, but everything she thought about reminded her of him. She knew she was smitten, but she didn't want to admit it to herself. She was too afraid of how she would feel if he didn't reciprocate the feeling. Yet in the back of her mind, she knew that they had just shared a moment that might change the tide of their relationship.

Moments Like These

Work was much improved since Brandt's reformation. Not only did she look forward to each new weekday, but their team effort was considerably more productive. Lunch had become the highlight of her day, since she joined Brandt at the sub shop across the street from their building. He had even offered to carpool with her. Since it was summer vacation, he drove every day because he had to drop Bridget off so Eve could watch her. One afternoon during a staff meeting, Jedidiah Corbett announced that Ainsley and Brandt would be attending a two-day training conference in Seattle, Washington.

Ainsley was packed and waiting on her porch when Brandt drove up in one of the city's fleet vehicles at 5:00 in the morning to pick her up for the conference the following week. The city had opted for an early departure rather than pay for an extra night for two hotel suites. The three-hour drive went by without a hitch. Conversation flowed naturally between the two, who were now accustomed to spending a little bit of almost every day in each other's company. They arrived with enough time to eat breakfast at a local diner and check into their rooms before the 9:00 classes began. They each attended different classes to get the most out of the training. Since lunch was catered, everyone ate in different shifts, so Ainsley never saw Brandt again the rest of the day.

When her classes ended, she returned to her room to try to figure out the glitch in the program she and Brandt had been working on. Suddenly, a light bulb clicked on, and she knew how the program needed to be modified. In her excitement, she walked across the hall to his room and knocked, still looking down at her notebook and the pile of papers she had in her hands. He opened the door almost immediately, and she noticed he had his jacket on as if he had been on his way out of the room.

"Oh, I didn't mean to bother you. I wasn't thinking. It must be dinnertime already, and you're headed out," she deduced.

"Yeah. I'm meeting up with some friends who happened to be at the training too. Is there something you needed?"

"Uh... no. It can wait. I think I figured out the glitch in our program, but ... um . . . see you tomorrow." She turned quickly on her heel and was back in her room before he could say a word in response, her face burning with humiliation. Of course, he would have plans. Most people probably didn't plan to work all evening, but he had the car keys, so she couldn't go anywhere except on foot.

She flipped through the stations on the TV and tossed the remote aside. Her stomach protested its long absence from food as she tried to remember if she had seen any fast-food chains near the hotel. She finally resolved to see what she could find, so she grabbed her coat. She was trying to get her hotel key into her purse as she opened her door and walked directly into someone. She shifted her head up to see who had been standing so close to her door when her eyes met

Brandt's.

"Going somewhere?" he asked amused.

"Yeah, I was just headed out for my nightly jog in the city," she replied sarcastically.

"In those shoes?" he asked as she looked down at her high heels.

"I thought I'd change it up a bit. I'm always up for a challenge," she quipped.

"I hear if one heel is taller than the other you get more of a workout," he commented, trying to conceal a smile.

"Oh, shut up," she said, shaking her head with a smile. "Will I ever live that down?"

"Not while I'm around," he answered, laughing.

"Why are you around, anyway? I thought you were on your way out a half hour ago."

"Out and back again. I just realized I had the keys to the car, and it's a long walk to get to the nearest restaurant."

"Hand over the keys, and I'll be out of your hair," she said holding the palm of her hand in front of him as she added, "Do you need a ride somewhere?"

"Not so fast. I've seen how you drive, and this car is checked out to me. I'm not about to let you wreak havoc on the streets of Seattle with my reputation on the line."

"So, what do you propose: a taxi or a rent-a-car?"

"How about chauffer services?"

"But what about your friends?"

"Oh, they're long gone by now."

"I'm sorry your night is ruined because of me. Really, I can just go to the convenience store on the corner and grab something. You'd probably still have time to catch up with them."

"Who said my night was ruined? Unless, of course, you have some devilry up your sleeve." Her heart skipped a beat, and the expression on her face had an unsettling effect on Brandt, who quickly added, "You don't have to come if you'd rather not."

"No, it's not that at all. I'm flattered. It sure beats spending the evening alone," she said. With that, they were off. He took her to a nice Italian restaurant and even paid for the meal.

As they were walking to the car after dinner, he asked, "Have you been to Seattle before?"

"Just once with my roommate, Liza. Her family lives here, but we pretty much never left her house. Deedra and I snuck out, so we could at least see the Space Needle while we were in town."

"Well, let me give you a tour of the town, then," he said as he opened the door for her. They drove around for a while, and then he stopped the car by a tree lined street.

"What's here?" she asked.

"It's a little park I like," he said, getting out of the car. She was already on the sidewalk before he came around to open the door. She followed him down the sidewalk next to a busy road for a while until he veered to the left. They walked through the trees until they came to a little pond that seemed to be secluded and sheltered from the outside world. It was quiet and calm. He sat down on the grass by the pond, and she did the same.

"I take it you've been to Seattle before?" she queried.

"Born and raised," he answered, "I lived here until just three years ago."

"What took you to Portland?"

"I needed a change of scenery."

"Or you were running away from someone?" she surmised.

"Not running away. . . more like starting over," he said, and she could tell he was trying to let her into his life in a way he hadn't before. He continued, "She left me. I came home from work one day to a note telling me Bridget was with my parents, and Malissa wasn't coming back. She was tired of living a lie. That's not really how I imagined my temple marriage ending, you know? She was one convincing liar in the beginning, that's all I can say. We had a rough go of it, but I was willing to stick it out for Bridget's sake. She didn't even say goodbye to Bridget – she just left. The next thing I heard from her was through an envelope in the mail with the divorce papers, granting me full custody of Bridget. A few weeks later, I saw her in town, hanging on the arm of a guy she dated before we were married, and I knew I had to leave. . ." his voice trailed off.

"I wish I could offer some sage advice or words of wisdom, but having never been married, I'm in the dark there," she tried to offer some type of encouragement, failing miserably.

"Why is that?" he probed. "Why aren't you married?"

"I've asked myself that question hundreds of times. Sometimes I think I must be invisible or maybe when I was born, I accidentally inhaled some male repellant or maybe I volunteered to be single in the pre-earth life or maybe I am emitting some odorless chemical that wards men off. When I was in high school the older ladies in my ward used to tell me I was the 'marrying kind,' as if that was supposed to comfort me on all the dateless Friday nights, all the dances I missed, all the phone calls I waited for that never came, all the wasted tears I shed that failed to summon my fairy godmother. The 'marrying kind' – what exactly does that mean? I secretly hoped it meant my situation would magically transform when I went to college, but it didn't – very few dates, even fewer phone calls, and more wasted tears. I watched roommate after roommate get married. I suppose that phrase of idle words – the 'marrying kind' – had been spoken by tongues full of pity and void of hope for me. I think I've resigned myself to the fact that I'll be an old maid, unless of course the monks suddenly change their celibacy vows, but even then, it would be a long shot," she chuckled and added, "my short answer would be that honestly, I don't know. I don't know what's wrong with me."

"Maybe it's not you – maybe it's them," he said. She noted that he excluded himself by saying them instead of us. Was he excluding himself from the pool of potential bachelors or was he trying to say that there was nothing wrong with him because he wanted to pursue a relationship?

"Oh well, that's neither here nor there," she said aimlessly, throwing a rock into the water. "This place is beautiful. I think it would make the perfect thinking spot."

"Precisely why I used to come here . . . but alas, the sun is gone, and we better head back." He got to his feet and offered Ainsley his hand to help her up. She grasped his outstretched hand, and at the touch of his skin on hers, she felt excitement roaring to life inside of her like an engine that has been idle for too long. It certainly wasn't the first time anyone had offered to help her up, but it was the first time she wished that particular someone wouldn't let go.

Ainsley learned that night that some wishes do come true after all because when she was on her feet, he didn't let go. She scanned the skies for the shooting stars that granted her wish, but she saw only thousands of little lights winking their congratulations at her. She chanced a glance at Brandt, who must have decided to do the same at precisely that moment because their eyes met as they walked under a dim streetlight. She saw him smile slightly at her, and she returned his smile with one of her own, her dimples animating it, revealing more than she would have liked.

A few steps more and they emerged from the solitude of the park that had silenced the sounds of civilization outside its perimeter. Ainsley could hear the honking horns, rushing traffic, and high-pitched beeping of the crosswalk signals, and she expected them to penetrate the bubble of happiness that surrounded her, breaking the spell. They did not, however, for it was Brandt's hand clasping hers from which the magic emanated. They walked in silence, but Ainsley was completely content. She pushed all thoughts aside from her head, so she could simply relish this moment – this moment for which she had waited a lifetime. When they reached the car, he let go of her hand to open the door for her.

"Thanks," she said.

"For what?"

"For taking me out tonight even though you already had plans."

"I can guarantee you were better company than those hooligans any day."

When she was back in her room, she wondered what exactly had happened tonight. He took her out for dinner, showed her his special thinking spot, revealed his past to her, and held her hand. He had actually held her hand! Her heart jumped several high hurdles at the thought of it. *He held my hand*, she thought, *but what does that mean?* Was it merely a friendly gesture? Was it an act of empathy since they had both revealed a secret sorrow from their past? Was it pity? Was it a romantic inclination? She certainly wasn't opposed to the latter since her feelings toward him had been altering by leaps and bounds lately, but was that his intention? She wrestled over all the possible implications until her mind finally succumbed to sleep.

The next morning, Brandt was his usual self, so Ainsley pretended to be her usual self as well, although she caught herself gazing in his direction far too frequently during their continental breakfast. She was struggling to focus on anything because the sound of his voice was distracting her. Luckily, they split up again during the training sessions. She didn't see him until it was time to leave the conference. Her bags were already packed when he knocked on the door.

The conversation on the drive back to Portland centered mostly on work. They had only a few loose ends to tie up before their project together was complete, and then she would return to the grants department. She dozed off during a lull in the conversation and was awakened by the car coming to a stop.

"Are we back already?" she said, disoriented.

"I hope you don't mind, but I took a little detour."

"To where?" she asked, looking around at the unfamiliar landscape.

"Mt. St. Helens," he answered as he shut his door and walked away. She got out of the car to stretch her legs and realized they were at a viewpoint that overlooked Mt. St. Helens, which was still quite a distance away. Brandt had walked to a small bench that faced the volcano and sat down. Having never actually been to Mt. St. Helens before, Ainsley was overcome by the sight. She stood by the car for several minutes before deciding to join Brandt on the bench to get a better, unobstructed view. She sat down quietly, not wanting to disturb his moment of solitude.

"Sometimes I feel like my life is like that mountain. Everything seemed fine, and then it just blew up in my face," Brandt's voice was low and serious, and his eyes stared blankly toward the volcano. Ainsley instinctively put her hand on his, which was resting on his knee, and gave it a little squeeze. The small gesture seemed like a natural source of comfort she could offer.

"Look at that gray valley that was leveled by the eruption and the floods that it triggered. It's still dead after all these years. We won't ever get it back. We can't turn back time and stop it from happening. It's gone, and we've just got to let it go, or we'll miss all the new life springing up around us like those trees on the hillside that have been replanted. The majority of them have taken root in spite of the ash and debris. I'll bet there's even a tree growing amidst the dead stumps as you get closer. Just a single tree but growing still. Even though the eruption was destructive, there's an element of beauty and serenity in it now. It's as if the blast calmed the mountain – changed the mountain – and in some ways, it's more majestic now. Before, it may have been just another mountain, but now it's respected and admired and awe-inspiring because we know how powerful it can be. We've seen its potential only because of its loss. I think life is like that too. We're passing through the refiner's fire just like the mountain has, and we'll come out stronger and more majestic too. . . with time." She had been thinking out loud as she looked at Mt. St. Helens, and as she finished her thought, she turned her head to look at Brandt.

She found his face just inches from her own, though she knew she hadn't been that close to him when she sat on the bench. Her heart suddenly launched into a full-speed sprint as Brandt stared into her eyes like no one had ever done before. He leaned in closer and closer until his lips pressed against hers. She never could describe the feeling she felt at that moment any more than she could describe the feeling she felt sitting on her parents' porch with a cup of hot chocolate, watching a snow blizzard in the dead of an Idaho winter or when she stepped outside, smelling the air after an Oregon rainstorm, or the great anticipation that curtailed her sleep every Christmas Eve when she was a child or when she watched her favorite romantic comedy or finished a really good book. It was all those feelings rolled into a ball into the pit of her stomach that erupted inside her with the gentle pressure of his lips against hers. It was the peaceful, joyous feeling of anticipation that left a person longing for more.

The kiss intensified for a moment, and then Brandt slowly pulled away, turning his head back toward the volcano, but holding her hand tightly in his, pulling her closer to him. She felt a flood of happiness surface on her face, leaving a smile in its wake. Ainsley had just experienced her first kiss at 28, and she couldn't help but feel that it was well worth the wait. No pimple-faced teenager could have managed a kiss like that and meant it the way Brandt Cragun had just done. She had to admit that it was even worth her first encounters with the former Mr. Road Rage. In fact, she appreciated the experience even more because she knew that Brandt didn't open up to just anyone.

They sat together on the bench for quite some time before he spoke, "I'm not sure what you've done to me, but I've never felt like this before." She could tell he had let his guard down with her. Where before he had been armored and protected, he was now vulnerable and exposed, and yet he still felt safe. He knew with her, his heart would be safe because it was as if his heart had been hers to protect and guard and love all along, at least that's how she interpreted the feeling.

"Well, it seems I tapped into some of your voodoo magic after all," he laughed at her comment, remembering her accusations the night she finally confronted him after the burglary.

"We better hit the road if we want to get back before it gets too late," he said as he pulled her to her feet. They walked hand in hand to the car. As he began to drive, he said, "You know this might be a little awkward for Bridget, so I think we'd better take it slowly."

"Well, I can assure you I've personally never gotten a ticket for speeding. Besides, I've always preferred the scenic route, which tends to take longer anyhow." Brandt smiled as he put the car into drive. When they reached a small KOA just a few miles down the road, he pulled off the road again and told her to wait in the car. As he emerged, she immediately recognized the logo on the large slush puppy cup.

"I haven't had one of these in years," she exclaimed as he handed her the cup.

"Consider it payment for mowing my lawn," he said as he buckled his seat belt. It seemed that she hadn't been the only one attentively watching and listening to her neighbor. How could he have possibly remembered that she fostered a slush puppy fetish from that one insignificant comment, unless...her thoughts trailed off to explore all the pleasant possibilities.

She decided not to tell anyone about what had happened between Brandt and her. This wasn't, after all, some teen romance, though it was her first. Their relationship was much more complicated than she had ever imagined it would be, and there was more at stake. He was divorced, and that made her uneasy. Ainsley didn't know exactly how he could ever stop loving the woman he had been married to for seven years, especially when she was the one who left him. She didn't want to feel like she was being compared to an ex-wife, particularly when she was so inexperienced herself. This had been the first time anyone had held her hand or kissed her, but Brandt had done that hundreds of times throughout the course of his courtship and marriage.

Then, there was Bridget. She was tangled in the middle of this delicate web by no choice of her own, and Ainsley didn't want her to be subjected to gossip or rumors of any kind. In addition, she certainly didn't know how her parents would react to her dating a divorced man with a 10-year-old daughter, particularly when that man happened to be Mr. Road Rage. Her mother was still suspicious of his sudden change of attitude toward her only child. But for now, she would simply relish the moments like these, without fuddling them up with worries about what might happen in the future.

Fireworks

The following work week was shortened by a day because of the Fourth of July. Liza was spending the holiday with Jim, and Corrin and Deedra were attending a family reunion, which left Ainsley by herself. She was obligated to go to the ward breakfast because she was in charge of some games for the older children. She assumed Brandt and Bridget would be spending the day with Brady's family, but he hadn't invited her yet. Their project had been officially completed, so she rarely saw him at work anymore, although they still met for lunch every day.

She had already ordered her sandwich and was sitting at a table by herself when she saw Brandt walk in. She was struck suddenly by how handsome he was. Her heart started to pitter-patter in her chest, and she couldn't conceal a smile from etching itself on her face. Although she had eaten lunch with him every day for the last three weeks, today felt different, probably because it was different. While she had noticed her feelings changing toward him, she hadn't known how he felt about her since he kept his feelings very much concealed. Last weekend, he proclaimed them loud and clear in a very amenable show of affection. His feelings almost felt stronger than her own, though she wasn't sure how that could be since he had seemed to detest her up until a month and a half ago. Now, there he was coming toward her, smiling at her with his half smile and his beautiful brown eyes. He was smiling at her in the way she had always dreamed someone would smile at her. She was afraid to blink, afraid he would vanish, and afraid last weekend was only a dream.

"Hey, you. Thanks for waiting for me," he greeter her.

"I wasn't sure if you were coming today. I'm not privy to your schedule anymore, you know," she deflected.

"Well, let's clear this up right now then. I don't think I could make it through a morning at work if I couldn't look forward to lunch with you," he said.

"I didn't know you felt so strongly about it. I thought it was that BLT that kept you coming back," she joked. The conversation died down while they both ate their sandwiches. Ainsley handed him one of her white chocolate macadamia nut cookies.

"So, any plans for the Fourth?" he asked, taking a big bite.

"Not really. It seems I'm home alone again. Imagine that. Well, after the ward breakfast, that is," she answered rather glumly.

"You're going to the ward breakfast?"

"I kind of have to. I'm in charge of some games for the kids. Why? Aren't you going?"

"I hadn't really planned on it."

"Great. So, I'm going to be stuck there by myself too," she said as she stacked her garbage on the tray.

"I suppose I could make an exception for you," he relented, tossing his garbage onto her tray too.

"Great!"

"But there's a catch," he interjected. "You'd have to come with me to Brady's for their annual barbecue."

"I guess if I have too," she pretended to be put out.

"I'll pick you up at 7:45 then, so we can get there before all the food is gone," he said while he emptied the tray in the trash. He held the door open for her, and they walked across the street to the city building where they parted ways.

The ward breakfast wasn't much to talk about. They went. They ate. They played a few games. They left, but at least Brandt and Bridget had been there with her, so she didn't have to endure it alone. The barbecue was much more exciting, as any activity with Brady and his family was bound to be. Brady laughed when she showed up with a salad even though Brandt insisted that she didn't need to bring one to appease Brady's sense of humor. The Cragun boys were like wild animals, and there was always some flourish of excitement and activity. When they were finished eating, Brandt and Brady disappeared into the house. Ainsley volunteered to bring the food in while Eve changed Kellan's diaper. The other kids were busy playing freeze tag.

Ainsley was taking a bowl of watermelon into the kitchen and happened to walk past the family room. The voices of Brandt and Brady stopped her before she reached the door, and she couldn't help but listen to their conversation.

"So, what are your plans for the rest of the night?" Brady asked.

"What do you mean? We're just hanging out here with you," Brandt replied.

"My house is no place for a proper date. You're going to drive her off if she has to stay here, and if you don't drive her off, you'll definitely ward her off from ever wanting children of her own. No, definitely not. You can't stay here. I'm officially kicking you out. Come on man . . . don't you remember how to date someone? Think about it. Would you have wanted to hang out with an old married couple and a bunch of kids when you first started dating someone – I mean before you had a kid of your own, that is? I never saw you hanging out with Grigg and his family when you were dating after your mission," Brady tried to persuade him.

"Brady, nobody would have hung out with Grigg and his family. I think mom and dad are still trying to figure out if he wasn't switched at birth," Brandt retorted.

"Seriously. You're going to screw this up. Why don't you take her to the fireworks in Vancouver?" Brady suggested.

"Since when did you become a love guru? Besides, I thought we were setting off fireworks here."

"Actually, since Dr. Love is in session right now, might I suggest you make some fireworks of your own, if you know what I mean?" Clearly Brandt understood his brother's meaning because Ainsley heard a scuffle followed by Brady's laugh.

"Brady, get a grip. I don't even know why I'm listening to you, and what about Bridget?"

"Quit hiding behind Bridget, Brandt. You already know the triplets have rented a tween movie to watch tonight. She'd probably quit talking to you altogether if you made her leave before she saw it. She's already planning on spending the night, and you're getting far too old for sleepovers at my house," Brady argued. "You never listen to me, and you always regret it. I hate to bring it up, but who tried to warn you not to get involved with Malicious?"

"Her name is Malissa. I don't want Bridget to hear you call her that. She's still her mother," Brandt warned.

"Malissa is a name for a decent, civilized human being, which that vindictive slut is not. I will not call her anything but what she is. She is a snake. You knew that deep down, but you let her charm you into thinking she was something or someone else." Ainsley almost dropped the watermelon bowl. She had never heard Brady speak so angrily, and it reminded her of her first encounter with Brandt.

"Brady, this is hardly the time or the place to discuss that. What's done is done. It can't be undone, and I'm not sure I'd undo it if I could."

"What are you talking about?"

"If I hadn't married Malissa, I wouldn't have Bridget, and Bridget is my whole life. If I had to do it all again just to have her, I would," Brandt explained.

"Point taken, but hear me out. Ainsley is not Malicious. Where Malicious is Antarctica, Ainsley is Hawaii. You yourself said that you've never felt this way about anyone before. I'm telling you – don't let her slip away. Be proactive, man. Go for it. You only get a chance like this once. If you won't do it for yourself, then do it for Bridget," Brady was clearly skilled in the area of pep talks. Ainsley was listening so intently that she found she was holding her breath in anticipation of what the conversation might reveal about the man she was coming to love.

"That's what worries me. I'm afraid I'm only thinking of myself when it comes to Ainsley."

"And you need to do that every once in a while – for Bridget. You know, it is called the great plan of happiness for a reason. You're entitled to be happy – you deserve to be happy. 'Men are that they might have joy'. . ."

"Okay, okay. Stop with the scripture citations already," Brandt interrupted.

"C'mon. The Fourth of July is about celebrating our freedom, isn't it? Take a night off and go celebrate your own freedom for once, will you? Freedom from the clutches of Malicious – freedom to love someone who actually deserves your

72

love. . ." Brady urged.

Just then, the back door opened as one of the kids came in from outside. Ainsley didn't want to be caught eavesdropping, so she popped her head right into the family room and said, "Any last-minute takers on watermelon before I put it away?" Brandt's face was as red as the watermelon as if he'd just been caught with his hand in the cookie jar.

"Have you been standing there long?" he asked.

"I just came in the back door," she lied. "Why? Did I interrupt some top-secret shenanigans?"

"No . . . I just didn't hear you come in," he said, unconvinced.

"Well, I can go back out and try it again with a little more gusto," she volunteered.

"No. We're finished in here anyway. I'll help you clean up," he said, ignoring Brady who was miming something behind him that Ainsley couldn't see. Brandt went outside to bring the rest of the salads and condiments indoors, while Ainsley put the watermelon in the refrigerator. When Brandt came back in, Ainsley helped him put everything away.

"So, would you be opposed to a little drive?" he asked Ainsley, unaware that Bridget was standing behind him.

"Where are we going?" Bridget asked as she reached for a cup by the sink.

"Well . . . I thought we could catch the fireworks in Vancouver," he proposed. Apparently, he had decided to take Brady's advice after all, love guru or not.

"Do I have to come?" Bridget whined as she crinkled her forehead in dismay.

"I guess not, if you'd rather stay here," her father said, visibly relieved by her reaction. The situation couldn't have played out better in his favor, and

Ainsley nearly laughed at how everything fell into place. She could practically hear Brady telling him, "I told you so."

"Yes!" Bridget exclaimed, clapping her hands together. "Traci and Teagan and I rented a movie we've been dying to see. Uncle Brady even offered to let us use his laptop, so we can watch it upstairs, alone. No boys allowed!" she bellowed as she finished her statement half way down the hall.

"So, what about you?" he asked again, turning to Ainsley, "Are you up for a drive?"

"Well, actually," she said, "I was hoping to watch the movie too."

"I see. I must be pretty bad company," he said, hanging his head as he pretended to feel rejected.

"I'm kidding. I'd love to go for a drive with you," she insisted.

"We better head out then," he said, grabbing her hand to escort her to the door. They said goodbye to Bridget and the rest of the Cragun gang with the children gawking at their Uncle Brandt, holding Ainsley's hand. Bridget just smiled.

"What happened to taking it slowly for Bridget's sake?" Ainsley asked as he opened her door.

"I am taking it slowly," he said as he unexpectedly leaned in to kiss her. The kiss was met with whoops and hollers from the gate as the children crowded to see what was happening.

"Way to go, Dad!" Bridget called out, as Brandt waved his hand at them, shooing them back into the yard.

"I see I'm going to have to put up some speed bumps, if this is taking it slowly," Ainsley noted as Brandt slid into the driver's seat, but she could tell that he only seemed more encouraged by Bridget's approval. Brady deserved a pat on the back because his little pep talk appeared to have enlivened Brandt quite a bit.

When they reached the site for the fireworks, Brandt paid and parked the car, extracting a blanket from the backseat. They walked to an unoccupied spot on the grass, which were few and far between since they had arrived so late. He sat down after he spread the blanket on the grass, and Ainsley sat down beside him. He draped his arm around her, and the scene reminded her of the night of the burglary when Brandt put his strong arms around her. She never would have imagined then that those arms would be wrapped around her again or that she would want them to be.

"This reminds me of going to the fireworks with my parents when I was a kid," she said as she took in her surroundings.

"Where are your parents now?"

"Still in Franklin, Idaho. Born and raised. They've already purchased their cemetery plots."

"And you don't have brothers and sisters?"

"Nope. Just me. Not that they didn't want to have more children, but after several miscarriages and a stillborn, they were happy with just me."

"And how do they feel about you dating someone like me?"

"Is that what we're doing? I thought this was our first date?'

"Officially maybe, but we've been holding unofficial rendezvous for two months now. You're dodging the question. What do they think?"

"Honestly, I haven't told them yet." He contorted his face with displeasure as she spoke.

"Oh? Afraid they wouldn't approve of you dating an old man?"

"Give me a break. You can't be that much older than I am."

"Why? How old do you think I am?"

"I'd say . . . early thirty-something," she guessed.

75

"Not bad. How about 35?"

"Oh my!" she mocked, "That old? I'm surprised you get around as well as you do. Maybe we ought to call it a night so you can make it home before your nine o'clock pill regimen."

"My age doesn't bother you?" he asked surprised.

"Why would it? You're only six years older than I am."

"But that means when I came home from my mission, you weren't even old enough to date by church standards."

"Well, it could hardly be considered robbing the cradle at 28, now, could it?"

"I guess not," he laughed, "but why haven't you told your parents about me?"

"Oh, they know all about you," she corrected. "I had to vent to someone the day of the accident, didn't I?"

"You're kidding me! They know about that? It's no wonder you haven't told them yet. They'd probably have the police escort you straight back to Idaho."

"My mom has threatened. . ." she laughed, "but I've also told them about your recent reformation."

"And . . ." he prodded.

"And the jury is still out. Mom's not as quick to forgive when her only child is involved. And I'm not going to lie to you. The fact that you're divorced with a child might not really meet my mother's expectations, but then again, she does live in her own little fantasy world, so it would be hard for any potential suitor to meet her standards."

"I see – I'm causing familial strife with all my baggage."

"Not at all. I tend to like you, baggage and all. My parents will come around too, once they get to know you like I do . . . and who couldn't help but love

Bridget?" she reassured.

"Bridget may be all I have going for me then."

"You've got me in your corner too," she assured him as she ran her fingers across the frown lines in his forehead. The music began, announcing the start of the fireworks show. He wasn't ready to end the conversation, and she could tell something was still bothering him.

"What's wrong?"

"I'm just curious. How do you feel about me being divorced?" She looked up to the sky before she responded.

"I'll admit, it's a little unsettling," he laughed, and she turned to look at him.

"Why are you laughing? I'm trying to be honest about how I feel, and you're laughing at me!" She could feel her face reddening.

"That's why I'm laughing. You're so brutally honest. It's one thing I've always liked about you. I never have to worry about you trying to deceive me. I never have to guess how you feel," his eyes reflected the light from the fireworks that had just lit up the sky. "Go on. I didn't mean to interrupt."

"Well, it makes me uncomfortable because I'm so inexperienced. I mean you were my first kiss, and I'm 28. Isn't that pathetic? And I just don't want to feel like I'm being constantly compared to someone else – someone I don't even know." He laughed softly at her again, shaking his head in disbelief.

"How do you get these silly ideas into that head of yours? Let me dispel your false notions right here and now. First, you're hardly pathetic. Virtue is never pathetic. Second, you can't even be compared to Malissa. You're so out of her league – so far superior to her in every way that I fear you're far too good for the likes of me. Third, that first kiss, if you don't mind my bluntness, was the best kiss I've ever experienced in my life. If that's what you consider inexperience, I hope to be around when you're experienced. I was afraid I fell short of what you may have imagined a first kiss to be like based on all those chick flicks from which you've probably molded your expectations," he pulled her close and kissed her again. And she understood what Brady had meant when he said they should make their own fireworks because a bottle rocket exploded inside her.

"Sir," she said in a low, disapproving tone, "this is a family friendly fireworks event." He smiled his half smile, revealing his dimple. She leaned close to his ear and whispered, "But let me assure you that the real thing, live and in person, is far better than anything I could have ever conjured up in my own head."

They were quiet as they watched the fireworks light up the darkening night sky. She rested her head on his shoulder, feeling as though she had been transported into a dream from which she hoped never to wake. On the drive home, there was a lull in the conversation, and Ainsley seized the opportunity to press him for the information she desperately needed to hear him say but had been too afraid to ask before.

"I didn't tell you the last reason dating a divorcee worries me."

"Oh?"

"Never mind," she mumbled, suddenly feeling stupid for prying into his personal life.

"C'mon. Just tell me," he urged.

"Well . . . do you still love her? Malissa, I mean?" she asked and quickly clarified, "I just don't understand how you can just stop loving someone, especially since she initiated the separation." He was quiet for a while before he answered.

"I thought I loved her for a long time, but I've realized that I don't even think I knew what love really was. I had become complacent about the situation. No . . . that's not it. I figured that's just how things were going to be, so I'd have to learn to deal with it because I couldn't change her. I looked passed things she did and said because I didn't want to know the truth. I wanted to live in my own little world where everything seemed okay – where there was a routine. Brady tried to talk to me about it more than once, but I didn't want to listen. I had been married in the temple after all, and temple marriages just don't end. I thought I was in love when we were married, and I wanted to love her for Bridget's sake, but now I'm realizing that it couldn't have been love. Or if it was, the person I thought I loved only existed in my head. If not for Bridget, I doubt I would have talked to her again after the divorce. I wasted seven years of my life trying to make everything okay only to lose it all in the end anyway. I know I gave it my best, and I also know our lives are better without her pulling us down in her constant web of lies and deceit."

"I'm sorry. I didn't mean to dredge up . . . well, I shouldn't have asked," she said, reaching over to touch his arm as he drove. He glanced at her.

"I'm glad you asked," he said, and she knew he meant it. While Vancouver's fireworks were being stowed away until another hot summer night in July, Ainsley's fireworks were still igniting as she drove home next to the man who had sparked them all to begin with – while the feelings he had so carefully buried three years before finally reached the surface to celebrate their independence at last.

On Sunday, Brandt invited Ainsley to attend a family home evening with Brady's family. Brandt and Bridget were in charge of the dessert, so that evening Ainsley joined them in making Bridget's famous chocolate chip cookies. On Monday evening, Eve gave a lesson about David and Goliath. She taught that we each had to acquire smooth stones of faith and testimony just as David had, so we could fight off temptation and sin. For the activity, everyone found a smooth stone and made a necklace out of it with wire and elastic cording.

Kellan, inspired by the story of David throwing stones, decided to take revenge on his own Goliath. At that moment, his Goliath happened to be Rylan, who was teasing Kellan with his stuffed puppy. He picked up a not so smooth stone that was sitting on the table, which turned out to be the arrowhead Thane had brought outside to show Brandt, and he threw it quite accurately for a two-year-old. The arrowhead hit its mark on the forehead, right below Rylan's hairline. When Rylan screamed out in pain, mass hysteria ensued as everyone tried to piece together what had happened.

Blood was pouring out of the open wound as Eve dashed into the house for a washcloth. Holden began to cry, yelling at Kellan, "You've killed him! You've killed him!" Thane was also yelling at Kellan for losing his arrowhead, for which he was desperately searching in the uncut grass. Kellan was crying because everyone was yelling at him, and his puppy was bleeding. The blood was actually from Rylan's wound, but there was no convincing Kellan that Rylan hadn't inflicted the injury. Ainsley and Brandt were trying to herd the children into the house to alleviate the congestive huddle around the whimpering Rylan.

"That'll teach you, son," Brady told Rylan. "It doesn't pay to be a Goliath. Just because someone is smaller than you, doesn't mean he can't draw blood. We weren't auditioning for actors to play Goliath tonight, you know."

Eve decided the cut was deep enough to require stitches, so she and Brady took Rylan to the hospital, leaving Ainsley and Brandt with the other six children. When everyone was finally calmed down, they ate dessert, and Brandt helped the boys get ready for bed. After a scripture story and prayer, the kids were tucked snuggly in their beds, and Ainsley flopped down on the loveseat in the family room.

"Well, that was certainly exciting," she announced, as Brandt sat down beside her.

"There's never a dull moment at this house," Brandt agreed. "I think Bridget would go absolutely crazy if she were stuck at my house all the time without all this commotion." Just then, Kellan appeared in the doorway with big tears running down his chubby little cheeks. He went straight for Ainsley, who picked him up.

"I sorry," he said in between sobs. "I wub Ry."

"I know you love your brother, and he knows it too," Ainsley reassured him as she stroked his hair. He was holding onto his puppy, which had been bandaged and kissed all better by the three girls. Ainsley moved to the rocking chair, so she could rock Kellan to sleep while singing the few Primary songs she could remember from her youth. He finally fell asleep forty-five minutes later, and Ainsley carried him to his room.

"You know, Kellan doesn't go to just anyone. He must really like you," Brandt said when she returned to the family room. "I was living with Brady and Eve just after he was born, and he still won't have a thing to do with me."

"That's not too surprising," she laughed. "You can come off as a little gruff sometimes."

"Thanks for helping me out tonight. You're a natural with the kids," he complimented.

"Now, let's not get carried away. I've always been a nervous Nellie around kids. When Brother Whitaker called me to be the activity day leader, my heart literally collapsed. That was the one place I didn't want to be."

"So, you don't like kids?"

"Oh no. I've just never been around them much. I didn't have brothers or sisters to take care of, and I wasn't a big fan of babysitting. My inexperience merely leads to discomfort. Who knows? Maybe that's why I was called to serve with children. The Lord knew I needed some experience that I wasn't going to get any other way." He looked away, and she could tell something was bothering him.

"What's wrong?" she asked, hoping she hadn't said something to offend him.

"You shared with me your reservations about dating a divorced man, so you must have qualms about walking into a ready-made family. You don't have time to ease into parenthood when there's already a ten-year-old girl thrown into the mix. You would have been eighteen when she was born," he was anxious as he spoke, and she could tell he had thought about the topic extensively.

"You know what's interesting? If you had asked me about that a year ago, I would have probably had a very different opinion on the matter. I've always wanted to have children of my own. Stepping into a family situation would have been terrifying to me, and I certainly would have shirked at the thought of it. But... how can I explain this to you? I was friends with Bridget before I was friends with you, and it's almost as if Bridget brought us together. I feel as though my life is better because she is a part of it...as though she is supposed to be a part of it somehow. I hope I don't overstep my bounds here, but I love her as much as I imagine I would love a child of my own," she was staring down at her hands as she spoke, and she was surprised when he put his arm around her and pulled her close to him.

"I'm glad she has someone like you in her life. You couldn't find a little girl more deserving of your love than her, especially after all she's been through," he said simply, and she knew her sincerity had pacified his fears.

Moments later, the door opened pronouncing the return of Brady, Eve, and Rylan, who had received three stitches. Brandt went upstairs to retrieve Bridget, who was already asleep in the twins' bedroom. Ainsley's heart swelled with unexpected emotion as she watched him carry his sleeping daughter in his arms so tenderly as he descended the stairs. At that moment, she knew she would never have to worry about whether he would be a good father because she could see that he already was. While there were many things she didn't know about him, she knew that he was a good man on more levels than one. She found herself anticipating a future with him and Bridget, which she never thought possible.

When they arrived at Brandt's house, Ainsley opened the doors for him as she did once before after a memorable evening at Brady's house for the soccer barbecue. She lingered downstairs instead of leaving straight away, although she wasn't really sure why. She felt as though their conversation wasn't yet at an end. Brandt was surprised to see her still sitting on the couch when he came back downstairs.

"You still here?"

"Ten o'clock isn't exactly my curfew, but I can leave if you need some alone time," she got up as if to leave, but he touched her arm to stop her.

"No, I was just surprised that you were still here, that's all. Last time you just left," he explained as she sat back down. He sat down next to her on the couch.

"You know, you're a really good dad," she blurted out. He looked at her quizzically, so she elaborated, "I mean, I sometimes think that you don't feel like you're a good father, but you are."

"Well, I appreciate that, especially coming from you, whose opinion of me wasn't so great not too long ago," he acknowledged. "I'm probably not the world's greatest dad like Brady is, but I do the best I can."

"Why do you compare yourself to Brady?"

"I've lived in Brady's shadow my entire life. He was always the gregarious one while I was more pragmatic. When we were younger, he made sure to include me in everything, even when I tried to hang back. He's a real people person. I used to joke around with him that instead of a snake charmer he was a people charmer. And kids adore him because he's such a goofball around them. Who needs the Pied Piper when Brady is around? I guess I just naturally compare myself to him."

"It's true your personalities are as different as your looks are alike, but different doesn't mean better. I hope you don't sell yourself short. I tend to like you just the way you are, and I may be biased, but I would have never dated a guy like Brady. He's one of those showboat types. Don't get me wrong. I have a great time when we're around Brady and his family, but I have an equally good time, if not better, when it's just the three of us – like last night when we were making cookies together..." she didn't finish her thought because she felt stupid for saying as much as she already had. When she turned to look at him, she found him staring at her with those deep brown eyes.

"A penny for your thoughts," she said to break the silence, which felt like it might suffocate her.

"I was just thinking about you, and how I've never felt as comfortable around anyone as I do around you. And about how crazy it is that you're sitting here beside me when five months ago I was swearing at you in a parking lot and wreaking havoc on your life," he told her.

"I have let you off the hook pretty easily, but you were willing to risk your life for me the night that burglar broke in, so I think we're probably square by now. Besides, maybe my life needed a little mayhem. You once told me it was all about perspective, right? I like my life from this perspective, past, present, and future," she said as his phone rang. As he got up to answer it, she said, "I better get going myself, anyway. We'll see you tomorrow." She slipped out the door before he could protest.

The next two weeks flew by, and most of Ainsley's free time on the weekends was spent in the presence of Brandt and Bridget. Whether at the zoo or the public swimming pool, Ainsley was having the time of her life. She also noticed that since their conversation about Brady, Brandt spent less time at Brady's house, and she hoped he hadn't gotten the wrong idea. Ainsley loved being around Brady and his family, but Brandt too often used Brady as a crutch, so she wasn't about to complain when Brandt decided to fly solo. Bridget didn't seem to mind either because it meant that she spent more time with her father instead of playing with Teagan and Traci all the time.

One of Ainsley's most memorable trips of the summer was the Friday she took off work to go on a one-night camping excursion to Silver Falls that Bridget and Brandt had planned. When they arrived late on Friday afternoon, Brandt set up two pup tents. Bridget and Ainsley were sharing the larger of the two. He grilled hamburgers on his portable propane grill, and they ate macaroni salad and potato chips until they were stuffed. Of course, they left room for roasted marshmallows over the campfire. Ainsley French braided Bridget's hair, while Brandt told stories of his own childhood camping expeditions with his family. Bridget's yawning increased, and Brandt finally sent her to bed. He ducked in the tent and tucked her in before returning to sit by the fire with Ainsley. He picked up her hand and ran his fingers across her forearm, tracing them over a horizontal red scab that branded her white skin.

"Been ironing again, I see," his comment was a statement rather than a question, which caught Ainsley off guard.

"How did you know it was from ironing?"

"You'd be surprised at how much I know about you from simple observation. One day I was driving by your house on my way to the grocery store, and I saw you in your living room window ironing. The next day at work, I noticed your arm. The thin slice of sheared skin reappears every so often."

"I can't help it if my iron has a grudge against me. Just out of curiosity, what else have you observed?" He shrugged his shoulders in response.

"Oh, come on. Just tell me," she insisted.

"For instance, you tuck your hair behind your ear when you're uncomfortable, even if it's already pulled back. You bite on your lower lip when you're thinking really hard. You curl your toes under your feet all the time, even in your shoes. When you don't understand something that I'm trying to explain to you, particularly at work, but you're pretending you do, you purse your lips ever so slightly and lower your left eyebrow. Your dimples only show if you're really happy or if you're being mischievous. Just to name a few."

"Well, if I didn't know better, I'd think I have myself an obsessed stalker," she said.

"Not a stalker," he rebuffed, "just a man who is unusually perceptive when it comes to a subject of great interest to him."

"Should I be flattered that you just referred to me as 'a subject of great interest?' You make me feel like I'm involved in some high-profile investigation in which I've just been named the person of interest, otherwise known as the perpetrator of the crime."

"Some people may say stealing someone's heart is a crime," he was only partially joking when he spoke.

"I suppose cupid isn't the most law-abiding citizen. Not only is he armed and dangerous, but there's the whole indecent exposure issue," she jested as she tucked her hair behind her ear.

"You see!" he exclaimed, pointing at her. "You're uncomfortable. You just tucked your hair behind your ear." She blushed, embarrassed she'd given herself away so easily. He leaned closer to her, turning her head toward him with his hand.

"Do I make you uncomfortable?"

"No," she answered. "It's me. I'm just not used to anyone talking to me like that. I get flustered, and then I start feeling self-conscious and stupid. I feel almost as if I've been transported into one of those romantic comedies, but everyone starts booing at me because I'm not acting the part correctly – because

I don't know what I'm doing. I know it sounds corny."

"Well, there's only one way to correct that," he paused while she contemplated a possible solution.

"Practice," he announced, and then he leaned close to her ear and whispered, "I think you're beautiful. I love your eyes and your nose and your lips." He traced her features with his finger as he spoke and kissed her on the lips. Then he added, "I like the fact that you're stealing my heart away, Ainsley."

"I wouldn't consider it stealing, if you're willing to part with it," she whispered back as he kissed her again. She certainly wasn't feeling awkward or self-conscious anymore. Maybe with a little practice she could acclimate to being the star of the Brandt Cragun Show. The fire crackled, though only deep orange coals were glowing in the pit. Brandt got to his feet, holding his hand out to help Ainsley up.

"Looks like it's time to hit the sack as my grandpa used to say," she said.

"Yep. We've got a long day of hiking ahead of us tomorrow," he agreed. She gave him a hug and added, "Thanks for the practice session." She crawled into her sleeping bag as she heard the coals sizzle in protest as Brandt doused them with water. She listened to the sound of the zipper to his tent open and close. Within what seemed like a few seconds, she heard the faint sounds of his light snoring.

The chirping and tweeting of birds awoke her the next morning. The night had been less than restful since Bridget was a snuggler. She was practically sleeping on top of Ainsley the entire night. Ainsley wiped the sleep out of her puffy eyes and reached for her watch. It was six o'clock in the morning. She knew there was no way she would ever get back to sleep, so she quietly wiggled out of her sleeping bag, grabbed her bag, and headed for the bathroom. She was glad to make use of the pay-per-use shower, which helped her push the grogginess to the back corner of her mind. She braided her wet hair, applied a dab of make-up, and headed back to camp. She found Brandt already collapsing his tent.

"You're quite the early bird," he noted as he saw her approaching. "How did you sleep?"

"Not as soundly as Bridget does apparently. She practically slept on top of me," she informed him.

"Oh, sorry. I probably should have warned you about that. She's been a snuggle bunny ever since she was little. She weighed only six pounds when she was born. I swear her whole body practically fit in the palm of my hand. When she'd wake up at night, I used to rock her back to sleep. She'd nestle her little fuzzy head right into the crook of my neck. I could feel her warm puffs of breath on my neck like a tiny whisper escaping in her dreamy sleep. I could hear every little snort and sniffle. We slept like that pretty much every night, so I'm probably to blame. I guess I trained her to snuggle from birth."

As he spoke, he gestured his story with his hand, holding out his palm as if a tiny baby were laying in it. Ainsley was struck by how tenderly he recalled the memories of his daughter and how his eyes twinkled, and his dimpled smile stretched across his face as he reminisced. She was swept away in his vision as he invited her to travel back in time with him.

"Ainsley?" his voice dragged her back to reality. "I'm not that captivating."

"Actually, you are," she countered. "I was just trying to picture you holding Bridget as a newborn. I guess in my mind, Bridget will always be frozen in time as a ten-year-old. It's hard to imagine her as a baby."

"The time passes too quickly, that's for sure."

"I get the sense that you were the nurturer of the family as well as the provider. At least I don't hear many stories of dad's getting up in the middle of the night to care for their babies when they have to get up to go to work the next day."

"I suppose pretty much everything in my life is atypical."

"I wouldn't necessarily call that atypical. I think it's more unique in an exceptional sort of way. I know I've told you this before, but you really are a great father. I love to watch you talk about Bridget because you always get this twinkle in your eye. My dad was never like that with me. He's not the kind of guy who expresses his emotions very easily. Bridget is fortunate to have you for a father." As if on cue, Bridget emerged from the tent, yawning.

"Can't a girl get any sleep around here?" she asked as she stretched her arms and legs. Ainsley laughed in response and started rolling up her sleeping bag. After their tents and chairs were packed in the back of the SUV, they ate breakfast, which consisted of Bridget's favorite raspberry filled powdered donuts and orange juice.

They set off on the Trail of Ten Falls, and Ainsley was mesmerized by the beauty of each of the different waterfalls, although her favorites were the Double Falls. The hike was intense at the inclines, and she hadn't been much of a hiker since her girls' camp days when hiking was required. There were several times she was sure she wouldn't make it the entire distance, but somehow, she managed, huffing and puffing along the way. Even with the physical strain, she was happier than she had ever been in her life. She felt complete for the first time, and she wanted to spend the rest of her life planning family vacations with Brandt and Bridget. Bridget even carved $A + B^2 = C$ on a bench while Brandt wasn't looking.

Bridget leaned over and whispered, "Look, Zee. Ainsley plus Brandt and Bridget equals the Cragun's." Ainsley smiled. They ate lunch near a creek, where they also waded and splashed in the cool water.

As they edged toward the last mile, Ainsley noticed an older woman struggling to help a young boy up the trail. Other hikers simply passed them by, but Ainsley knew the woman would never get out of the park before dark at her current pace. As she approached the duo, she asked, "Is there anything we can help you with?"

"My grandson tripped over a rock a while back and hurt his ankle. I don't think it's broken, but he can't put any weight on it," the woman explained.

Brandt had come up behind them after stopping to snap a few photos. After hearing the woman's dilemma, Brandt took his backpack off his shoulders, handing it to Ainsley. Luckily, they already drank most of the water it had contained, so it wasn't too heavy.

"I'd be happy to carry him the rest of the way," he offered. The woman's eyes filled with tears, and she nodded her head because she couldn't speak. Ainsley helped the woman maneuver the boy onto Brandt's back. She knew it must have been a strain since the boy had to weigh at least 50 pounds, but Brandt nonchalantly continued up the trail, striking up a conversation with his new passenger. Bridget followed her dad, and Ainsley brought up the rear after the woman. Several times, the woman tried to talk to Ainsley as she walked, but her eyes misted over instantaneously, so she kept walking in silence. When they reached the trailhead, the woman called out to a bunch of teenage boys playing volleyball on a large open grassy area. They rushed over and helped the younger boy dismount from Brandt's back. They carried him to a picnic table, where several adults crowded around him.

"How can I ever thank you?" the woman asked. "I stumbled along for an hour with him, and not one person stopped to help me. I was beginning to wonder how we would ever make it back when you came along. Thank you so much. I hope my grandsons grow up to be men like you. God bless you and your family." She hugged Brandt, Bridget, and Ainsley in turn before she walked back to her family.

"Wow! Service in action," Bridget exclaimed approvingly as they walked to the SUV. Another weekend ended with an affirmation of Brandt's good character and Ainsley's growing attachment to him. Ainsley became all too comfortable in her new routine, which incorporated as much of Brandt and Bridget as possible. The days of the next week sped by far too fast. Before she knew it, the last weekend of August was upon her, which happened to be her 29th birthday – the last mile before she reached the crest of the hill that represented the passing of another decade of her life.

Swept Off Her Feet

Conveniently enough, all of Ainsley's roommates seemed to disappear every Saturday at precisely the designated cleaning time with every excuse imaginable. Ainsley donned her earbuds and started cleaning the house even though it was her birthday. She was busy cleaning the interior of the garbage can, practically crawling into it with her rear end protruding from the opening, waggling along with the music. When she was finished, she turned around to throw the paper towel in the garbage sack by the entrance to the kitchen and screamed. Brandt was leaning against the door jamb with his arms folded, his lips drawn into an amused smile. Ainsley paused her music.

"What are you doing?" he asked with a chuckle.

"Saturday's work, of course. Just because it's my birthday doesn't mean that the little fairies are going to clean for me, you know. Although there must be a bit of magic at work around here because my three roommates seemed to have vanished into thin air," she answered.

"I meant, what were you doing in the garbage can?"

"My mom always says, 'Your house is only as clean as the inside of your garbage can.'"

"Interesting. . ." he mused.

"What are you doing here, anyway?" she asked.

"Besides watching your dirty dancing?" he quipped.

"Real funny - unless my watch stopped, you're nine hours early for our date."

"There's been a slight change of plans tonight," he explained. "I tried calling, but you wouldn't answer your phone. I'll be by to pick you up at six instead of seven. Bridget planned a little surprise for you." She instinctively lifted her arm to run her fingers through her hair but was stopped short by the pile of sponge curlers on her head. She had completely forgotten she had them in, and she imagined she looked absolutely ridiculous to him, although he made no mention of it.

"Can't wait to find out what it is," she said, pushing him out the door. "Now, shoo." She ran to a mirror to see what damage had been done. She looked like Medusa's twin sister.

"Oh well," she muttered under her breath as she continued cleaning. He clearly hadn't been turned to stone yet.

Several hours later, Ainsley was sorting through her closet trying to decide what she should wear, when she suddenly realized that all her dresses looked like attire straight out of a sister missionary's suitcase. No wonder no one ever noticed her. She might as well have strapped on the black name tag and branded herself off limits for the rest of her life. Just then, Deedra burst through the door.

"Zee! Don't do it!" she screamed.

"Don't do what?" Ainsley inquired as she jumped at the sudden intrusion.

"Don't even think about wearing anything out of that closet!"

"What are you talking about?"

"Girl, you are not going out in Molly Mormon attire."

"What do you suggest then?" Ainsley asked as Deedra slinked out the door, reappearing with a wrapped gift box.

"The girls and I pitched in to get you a little something special," she said, smiling from ear to ear. "Happy birthday!" Ainsley ripped off the wrapping paper and opened the box. She pulled out a long black dress with an empire waist, square neckline, and a sheer green overlay embroidered with dark green leaves that matched the shade of Ainsley's eyes.

"Oh," Ainsley gasped, "it's beautiful! This looks way too expensive. I can't accept it." Ainsley tried to refuse the gift, but there was so much longing in her voice that Deedra only laughed at her.

"Whatever! I got a great deal on it, so just try it on!" Ainsley did as she was directed.

"I am so good," Deedra bragged as she went in search of the perfect pair of matching shoes in Ainsley's closet.

"Bingo," she exclaimed, tossing out a pair of black high heels. "Now sit down, and let me work my magic," Deedra commanded as she rubbed her hands together, and Ainsley knew that resistance was pointless. Deedra left her hair long, flowing, and unusually curly in the back with the sides drawn up in some sort of twisting knots through which she had woven sheer black ribbon. As Deedra sprayed another round of hairspray, the doorbell rang. Ainsley didn't have time to look herself over before going downstairs to answer the door, but she knew from the thoughtless stupor on Brandt's face that Deedra had indeed worked her magic very well.

"I feel a little under dressed," he said, tugging at his suit coat.

"You did say the dress was formal?"

"That I did, and you look remarkable in formal. Shall we?" he offered his arm to her as they walked to his SUV. When they arrived at Brady's house, she was escorted straight to the backyard where the gazebo had been decorated with twinkling Christmas lights. A small round table sat in the center with several candles lit in the center. Bridget was waiting expectantly as they approached.

"Good evening, sir," she said nodding toward Brandt. "Good evening, madam. I'll be your hostess tonight. May I get you something to drink?" she asked as Brandt pulled Ainsley's chair out for her.

"Water, please," Ainsley said.

"I'll have that right out to you, and here are your menus." She handed them each a handmade menu, drawn in crayon and marker. Ainsley was still admiring Bridget's creativity when she emerged a few minutes later with the waters.

"We have only one entrée tonight, but it comes highly recommended. Would you like soup or salad with your dinner?" Bridget asked.

"I'll have the salad," Ainsley responded.

"Make that two," Brandt echoed.

"Very well. Your meal will be right out." The service was very prompt since she returned only a minute later, with Traci and Teagan in tow, carrying two salads and two plates of baked lasagna rolls. As soon as the food had been delivered, the three girls disappeared again into the house. After several bites, Ainsley glanced over at the window and smiled when she saw seven pairs of small eyes peering through the lower portion of the family room blinds with two pairs of adult eyes peeping through the upper portion.

"Looks like we've got company," she whispered, moving her eyes in the direction of the window. Brandt glanced in the same direction.

"Maybe we should give them a little show," he suggested, raising his eyebrows.

"I think a little wave ought to do the trick," she responded as she turned to wave at the window. The blinds immediately snapped shut, and no one was seen looking through them through the rest of dinner. They finished their meal, which was better than any she had eaten in a restaurant. The waitresses rushed out to clear their plates from the table.

"Have you saved any room for dessert?" Bridget asked, pulling out a notebook.

"Certainly! What do you recommend?" Brandt asked.

"Ah – so many choices," Bridget said, "but the house special tonight is very good, so I am told."

"Two house specials, it is then," Ainsley ordered.

"Coming right up," Bridget said as she refilled their water glasses. A few minutes later she appeared with two slices of ice cream cake made with oatmeal cookie crunch ice cream.

"I hope it is to your liking, madam."

"Oh yes, very much so! May I ask how you knew this was my very favorite dessert ever?" Ainsley asked.

"Deedra is very easily persuaded," Bridget laughed, sounding very grown-up indeed. Turning to her father, she asked, "Are you ready for your check, sir?" He nodded, and she produced from her black apron a black folder, which she handed to Brandt. She promptly left upon delivering the bill as Brandt read aloud, "Two orders of baked lasagna rolls with a side of salad, two glasses of water, and two ice cream cakes. Total: Free for the young lady's birthday present. Tip preferred but not required." They both laughed.

"Might I suggest a $5 tip for each waitress? It's the best service I've ever had," Ainsley recommended.

"Feeling a little generous since it's not coming out of your pocketbook, are you?' he quipped, but he pulled three $5 bills out of his wallet and placed them in the black folder.

"Thank you!" Ainsley called out to the deserted back porch as Brandt pulled her chair out for her and escorted her to the gate.

"Now where?" Ainsley asked as Brandt backed out of the driveway.

"I thought a little dancing might be in order."

"Dancing?" she croaked as her eyes widened with dread. "No, no, no, no, no, no, no. That is not a good idea."

"Why not?" He was amused rather than deterred by her reaction.

"Because I can't dance, that's why not," she insisted. "Oh, please. I'm begging you – especially in front of other people. You'll be so embarrassed, and I'll have to call Deedra for a ride home."

"Who said anything about other people? Besides, you're out of luck. You already agreed to this. That's as good as a contract in my book, and there are serious penalties for breach of contract," he advised, having anticipated her reluctance.

"Well, if you put it that way, I don't have much of a choice, do I?"

"That's more like it." When the SUV stopped, she was surprised to find they were outside of his house. He hopped out of the car to open her door.

"I'm not sure I understand what's going on," she said, but he didn't offer an explanation. He opened the front door to reveal his living room, cleared of all furniture. It was just a hardwood floor and several hundred clear Christmas lights roped around the ceiling and down the walls.

"I see you've been busy," she observed, stepping across the threshold.

"Welcome to the Cragun School of Ballroom Dance," he said with a bow.

"I've entangled myself with a man of mystery. I didn't know you could dance."

"I needed electives in college, and Brady dared me to sign up for ballroom dancing. I've never been known to back down from a dare, so I did it. I didn't anticipate actually liking it, however. But I really enjoyed it, so much in fact that I dared Brady to take it the following semester, which he did. That was where he met Eve."

"Impressive – but I really can't dance."

"You just have to have the right teacher. Now quit stalling. This is only a pit stop."

"I'll do it. . . only for you, but you have to promise me that if I'm no good, you won't make me dance in public – and keep it simple."

"Deal," he concurred. With that, he started the music. He proved to be a very good teacher. She found dancing much easier when she just let him lead, although there were several crushed toes and near misses throughout the course of the lesson. She loved the closeness of his body to hers, the feel of his hand on her back, the touch of his skin, and the rhythm and flow of the music. She loved it all. She loved staring into his eyes while not saying a word. She loved examining every detail of his face from the tiny scar that cut into his right eyebrow to the shape of his nose to the curve of his lips. She loved the feel of his minty breath across her forehead as he breathed in time to the music. She loved his smell and the smell of the house. The aromas reminded her of the night of the burglary when she slept on his couch. It was the smell of protection, safety, and comfort. The music stopped all too soon.

"Well, Miss Nelson, I think you're ready for your debut. How about it?"

"If you're sure I won't make a fool of myself."

"You're a natural," he reassured her.

"But there's something missing," he said as he tapped his finger on his chin.

He left the room and emerged with a small box, which he handed to her. She opened it with trembling hands and found a necklace on a 14-karat gold chain. From it dangled a heart-cut emerald obsidianite stone. She looked up at him in search of an explanation. He took the necklace and walked behind her to put it around her neck.

"The stone was made out of the volcanic ash of Mt. St. Helens. Some people refer to it as Helenite. When the ash is heated to extreme temperatures, it's transformed into this translucent green glass," he explained as he shifted her hair to one side so he could fasten the clasp. "When I met you, my heart was just a pile of ashes blowing with whatever wind churned it up, but you somehow managed to gather all that ash and mold it back into a heart for me, which was something I never thought I would have again. The green color reminded me of your eyes, but it also reminded me of the trees springing back to life after the disaster. You are my tree seedling, growing despite the ash, and giving me back my life as you do. Thank you," he said as he kissed the back of her neck, sending tingles rushing down her spine and raising goose bumps on her arms.

She turned around to give him a hug, unable to speak. No one had ever given her such a heartfelt gift before – such a personal and thoughtful emblem of his feelings, as well as their first intimate moment together. He leaned down, drawing her lips into a kiss.

She was sure he was somehow re-routing her entire nervous system with a heightened response to the touch of his arms around her while his lips caressed hers. Her heart began racing blood through her veins in every direction at full throttle. They had both been magnetized to each other, and neither could pull away. She had never before felt these sensations – the deep yearning to be closer to him still. A red alert went off in her head as she edged closer to the boundary she had constructed to keep her virtue intact. She would not cross that line. She mustered enough strength to pull away, and he didn't resist. Instead, he pulled her into a hug, and she could feel his heart beating as if it were dancing the Lindy Hop. *I love you*, she thought, *oh, how I love you*, but she couldn't find her voice to speak the words. A honk from the driveway made Brandt jump, and he quickly released her.

"That would be the next phase of the journey," he announced as he walked toward the door, which he opened just as Brady was lifting his hand to knock. "Thought I'd give you a little warning before I came in – didn't want to interrupt anything," Brady said loudly enough for her to hear. He winked at her, which made her face burst into virtual flames. He only laughed at the confirmation of his suspicions.

"Would you leave her alone? I've only just barely convinced her to go with me, and I don't need you changing her mind," Brandt pretended to scold his brother. Ainsley joined Brandt by the door and followed him to Brady's car. As they sat in the back seat, Brandt grabbed Ainsley's hand.

"No hanky-panky in my back seat," Brady called out.

"Why don't you use your rearview mirror for driving instead of spying?" Brandt retorted.

"Boys," Eve said in her best motherly tone, "that will be quite enough of that. Why don't you act your age?" Ainsley laughed at the all too familiar banter among them, content to feel like a part of their family. They drove to an old dance studio, which had been renovated into a nice dance hall. There they danced the night away until Ainsley thought her feet might just offer their resignation. She had never had such an enjoyable birthday in her entire life, and she often found her fingers fumbling with the heart pendant that hung around her neck. When the evening was over, Brady dropped them off in Ainsley's driveway, and Brandt walked her to the front door.

"Now that wasn't so bad, was it?"

"It was great. Thank you for making me go."

"You're very welcome."

"And thank you for the necklace. It really means a lot."

"Not as much as you mean to me." He bent down to kiss her goodnight.

"Goodnight, Brandt," she whispered as she opened the door. She shut the door and slid down with her back against it until she reached the floor, too exhausted to move. *So, this is what it's like to be swept off my feet*, she thought with a sigh.

9

Detours

After her birthday, Ainsley found herself at Brandt's house every night. One of the three of them was always coming up with an excuse for her to come over. On one occasion, Bridget called to ask if Ainsley would come over to teach her how to French braid her own hair. She ended up eating dinner with them, as well as reading scriptures and having family prayer. After Bridget had gone to bed, Brandt challenged her to a Wii game. And so it was every night after work in addition to the weekends. If they weren't playing a game, attending one of Bridget's games, or watching a movie while curled up on the sofa together, then they were talking on the back deck about anything and everything. Brandt's little two-person family fit Ainsley like her favorite pair of jeans. She was more comfortable and happier than she had ever been. Although they spent more time together than they ever had before, they had much less physical contact aside from holding hands and an occasional good night kiss. Anything more than that seemed to ignite fires that neither of them was very good at extinguishing.

They still had family home evening every Monday with Brady's family, and Ainsley loved it when it was their turn for the lesson or activity. The three of them would spend Sunday afternoon planning together, and they often had insightful and fulfilling gospel discussions.

Once Brandt opened his heart to her, he didn't try to mask his feelings. He was very forthright about how he felt, and his actions announced it to the world. When he loved, he loved with all his heart, holding nothing back, except verbalizing the three little words that would confirm what she already knew. He had left his heart in the open - unguarded and unprotected - which was exactly how it had been broken in the first place. Now, even as it was beating again for the first time since its last attacker struck her near fatal blow, Ainsley found it quivering and afraid, reluctant to verbally commit to love again, though it was already too late to turn back without suffering a fatal wound from which there would be no recovery.

His hesitance was the fear of one who had lost much in the war of life on the battlefield of the heart, bugling loudly for its master to retreat, to run away, to cower, though no enemy advanced except the ghost army of pain and memories. Yes, the ghost army was still attempting to wage war with its battle cry from the past, demanding the surrender of all happiness, present and future. That war, that conflict constantly tormented Brandt as he commenced his march to reclaim the ground he had lost and to at last declare victory where he had once succumbed to defeat. However, he had yet to find his voice because it was still stifled in the roars and shouts of his ghost army, which choked the sound with its threat of returning to lay claim on his present and future.

Ainsley had never told him that she loved him either mostly because she knew he couldn't reciprocate the sentiment, not yet at least. If she had done so, his response would have been an awkward silence. She didn't want to provoke any uneasiness between them, and she wasn't about to push him faster than he was willing to go. After all, she had waited for him for so long, nearly abandoning hope of finding someone to love and someone who would love her in return. What was a little more time? She tore the page for the month of September off her calendar with a happy sigh.

Brandt didn't show up for lunch the following Friday, and when she tried to call him later that evening, he didn't answer his home phone or his cell phone. Worry began to niggle at the back of her mind. She hadn't seen him since Thursday's lunch at the sub shop. On Saturday morning, Ainsley still hadn't heard from him, and she noticed that Eve's van was in the driveway. Under the guise of delivering a temple print that Bridget had done during her last activity day, Ainsley knocked on the door. Eve answered.

"Oh, hi, Ainsley. Brandt's not here, but I'm sure you already knew that since he went to Seattle for work again," Eve said.

"Actually, he didn't mention anything to me about going to Seattle," she confessed as her stomach lurched to her toes at the unexpected news. "I just came by to drop this by for Bridget," she handed the temple print to Eve. "I don't know if you have any plans or not, but I was going to see if Bridget wanted to come over this morning to finish her dad's birthday present that we've been secretly working on together."

"We just dropped by so she could pick up her swimming suit, but we weren't planning on going until this afternoon. The kids have been bugging me to go to the indoor swim park for weeks now. I'm sure she'd love to spend the morning with you. I'll just swing by and pick her up around 1:00 for swimming." Someone was now honking the van horn incessantly, so Eve darted out the door, leaving Ainsley to wait for Bridget.

Bridget and Ainsley spent the rest of the morning putting Brandt's birthday scrapbook together. By the time Eve arrived to pick Bridget up, the scrapbook was complete, except for the ribbon, which Ainsley was going to have to buy. She promised Bridget that she'd finish it up and bring it over before Brandt's birthday the following week. Since she had nothing better to do, she went to the store to get the ribbon later that afternoon. Her cell phone rang while she was checking out. Brandt's home number flashed across the screen, making her heart flutter to life. Her hand was shaking nervously as she answered.

"Hello?" she tried to sound casual even though she was sick to death about his mysterious departure.

"Hi, Ainsley. Hey, I need to talk to you before Bridget gets back. Can you come over?" his voice betrayed nothing of the impending conversation.

"Sure. I'm on my way home now. I'll be there in about ten to fifteen minutes," she replied.

"Okay, we'll see you in a few then." There was nothing but dial tone and a million what-if scenarios buzzing around in Ainsley's head like a swarm of killer bees stinging her newly acquired sense of contentment and stability.

She knocked once on his door, and then let herself in. The minute she looked at him, she knew something was wrong. It was the feeling she got when dread and fear decided to bungee jump through her intestines, while worry set up a slippery slide on her insides, beginning at the throat and ending at the pit of her stomach. She did not like the way he looked at her one bit. She walked closer to him, putting her hand on his shoulder hesitantly, and for the first time in months she felt unsure of herself around him.

"What's wrong?" she asked.

"I can't do this," came his somber reply. His words were a point-blank shot to her heart.

106

"But why? What happened? What have I done?" she asked as she withdrew her hand and stepped away from him. There was no idle chit chat, no beating around the bush – he just pulled the trigger.

"You haven't done anything. It's not you…" he began to say.

"I get so sick and tired of hearing that. Why do people think they can package up these trite little phrases disguised as comfort and deliver them to me at the most inopportune times to miraculously make things all better? Here's one for you: I thought you were different."

"Ainsley… please."

"Please what, Brandt? If you have something to say, just say it for heaven's sake! Shed some light on the subject for me because I'm completely in the dark here," she pleaded.

"You wouldn't understand," he muttered.

"Oh, keep the clichés coming; it's clearing everything right up for me. In fact, it's as clear as mud. And you're right. I'll never understand because you won't trust me enough to tell me. Just tell me, please. Whatever it is, we can work it out together."

"I'm sorry. I didn't mean to hurt you." She could tell he had already made up his mind, and no amount of arguing or reasoning would alter his decision. "I just think this would be for the best . . . for all of us." She felt tears trying to surface as she attempted to blink them back unsuccessfully.

"Please don't presume to know what's best for me. Hurting me is one thing, but Bridget…" she didn't finish the sentence, knowing full well that hurting Bridget wasn't his intention. She knew that in his own twisted, contorted mind, he thought he was trying to protect Bridget, and maybe he thought he was protecting her as well. She wiped at her tears with a trembling hand as he looked away from her.

"Brandt," she added, "it doesn't have to be like this. You know that already though, don't you?" Brandt had turned his back toward her, but she continued, "Pushing me away isn't going to solve whatever problem you're trying to solve. Crawling back in your cave alone won't spare anyone's feelings, if that's what you're trying to do. Before I go, I just want you to know the one thing I've wanted to tell you for a long time now, but I was waiting for you to make the first move. I see your move wasn't exactly what I was anticipating, but I can't leave without saying it whether you reciprocate the feeling or not."

"Ainsley, whatever it is, please don't," he interrupted without turning around to face her. "Just go, please." His voice was a low, soft pleading that was so pathetic she obeyed out of sheer pity. As she walked out the door, Eve drove up with Bridget, who jumped out of the minivan and threw her arms around Ainsley's waist. Ainsley took a deep breath to get her composure, so Bridget wouldn't see her crying.

"Hey, kiddo," she hugged her back as Brandt came onto the porch, running his fingers through his hair.

"How was swimming?" she asked.

"It was the greatest! I dove off the high board for the first time ever!" she said excitedly.

"You did? Well, that is one accomplishment that deserves a trip to the ice cream shop," Ainsley said trying to smile.

"I bet we could go right now. Hey dad –" she called to her father, but Ainsley put her hands on Bridget's shoulders and bent down so they were eye level.

"Let's just make this one between you and me, my special treat, okay? But I have to be somewhere right now, so maybe I could pick you up tonight," she offered.

"Sure," Bridget agreed and then called out, "Hey, dad, is it okay if I go with

Zee tonight for some ice cream?" Ainsley turned around, awaiting Brandt's response. Whatever happened between them, Bridget would never feel the brunt of it if Ainsley could help it. Brandt smiled approvingly at Ainsley, silently thanking her for her chivalry, though sadness still clung to his eyes. She did not return the smile.

"Sure," he called back.

"Okay, then. Come over to my house at 7:00." She kissed the top of Bridget's head and walked across the lawn, suddenly feeling like a zombie. She went straight to her room, closed the door, and collapsed on her bed. Her life had just been given a shot of Novocain: one minute she could feel everything, anticipating every heartbeat, every sensation, and now she was numb. She felt nothing. Even her deeply dug well of tears was completely dry.

Later that evening, Ainsley found herself sitting across from Bridget at the ice cream parlor, but Bridget wasn't her usual bubbly self. She was poking at her ice cream with her spoon.

"What's up?" Ainsley asked, knowing full well that she couldn't avoid the conversation forever.

"So, you and my dad had a fight?"

"Is that what he told you?" Ainsley felt anger crawling up her spine like an army of fire ants ready to attack.

"Well...not exactly," Bridget confessed. "But I'm not stupid. He and my mom didn't exactly get along."

"I think your dad has something on his mind, and he needs some time to work it out for himself," Ainsley offered the only explanation she had, though she knew it was hardly soothing.

"Does it have anything to do with his trip to Seattle?" Bridget asked, attempting to launch her own investigation.

"I really don't know, Bridge. He didn't tell me exactly what was bothering him."

"Typical," Bridget muttered as she stirred her melting ice cream. "All he told me was not to worry about it – that it had nothing to do with me. But it has everything to do with me. He just doesn't get that. I liked how things were," she was trying not to cry as she avoided Ainsley's eyes by becoming suddenly interested in something at the cash register.

"Your dad has his reasons, I suppose, but don't think for a minute that anything will change between you and me, okay? Maybe we'll have more time alone together to do girl stuff. Now, try to cheer up, and eat your ice cream before it's completely melted." Ainsley ate a spoonful of her ice cream, but she tasted nothing. She was still numb, and all her senses were dulled. She didn't know how to console Bridget because she had yet to find her own consolation. Her heart broke even more than she thought was possible as she watched a tear escape Bridget's eye. They finished the rest of their ice cream in silence. When they arrived home, she gave Bridget a hug before watching the little girl, who had somehow woven herself into Ainsley's life, walk dejectedly across the lawn to her front door.

At church on Sunday, Bridget nestled beside Ainsley on the bench, but Brandt hung back, choosing instead to sit in the back row with Brother White and Brother Harris, the two widowers of the ward. Ainsley could feel the ripples of gossip and speculations descending upon her once smooth lake of happiness, but she pretended all was well. She was going to have to become a great pretender to pull this off, but she knew she couldn't hold out forever. Something was going to give sooner or later. Maybe it hadn't been so smart to get involved with her next-door neighbor and co-worker. There was simply no way to avoid him. He was everywhere. Her escape came quite unexpectedly, however, the following morning. Jedidiah Corbett summoned her to his office, not too long after her arrival.

"Ms. Nelson, the city of Seattle is interested in learning about your integration program, so Brandt has arranged for an employee swap which would allow us to tap into some of their knowledge on the new budgeting software they have just implemented. This is highly unprecedented but mutually beneficial for both city governments. You've done such a splendid job on the project," he explained.

"You want me to go to Seattle? But what about all my grants' work? I have so much to do because I spent so much time on that project, and it was just as much Brandt's project as it was mine," she tried to excuse herself from the assignment.

"Not to worry. We've had several requests from students for unpaid internships to fulfill their volunteer work requirement for the governmental accounting class, so we've arranged to offset your workload with them. And Brandt was the one who recommended you for the swap. It's only for six weeks, and I really hope you'll accept. We've arranged for housing as well. One of Brandt's contacts in Seattle has a roommate who left unexpectedly for an internship in New York, and you're welcome to stay there free of charge since rent was paid in advance." Ainsley was speechless – six weeks living in Seattle with people she didn't even know! He was unbelievable! He had stooped to a new low, far below anything Mr. Road Rage had ever managed. He must have been desperate to get away from her, causing as little inconvenience to himself as possible. Of course, he would give her the boot, and she supposed she should have expected as much given his abrupt about-face concerning the relationship he instigated. She wouldn't be surprised if she found her bags packed and a taxi waiting to usher her out of the city when she stepped outside the building.

"When would I leave?" she asked.

"They'd like you there on Wednesday, if at all possible. I know it's short notice, but they've got to be in compliance by the end of the year. Today, I want you to fill Debbie in on where you are with the grants, so she can take over. Tomorrow you can drive up there. We'll reimburse the mileage. Oh, and here's the address of the apartment," he said as he handed her a piece of paper with an address in Brandt's handwriting. "She's expecting you tomorrow afternoon."

"Okay, then," she mumbled as she walked back out the door, furious that she hadn't even been given a choice in the matter. She had just been pushed from her air-conditioned bubble of comfort and happiness into the sweltering heat of heartbreak and loneliness that sucked the very breath out of her.

As she packed that night, she replayed her conversation with Brandt in her head for the millionth time, searching for new clues that would help her unravel his mysterious departure from her life. Something had made him recoil, and it wasn't something she had done. In fact, she was fairly confident it had nothing to do with her at all, and everything to do with a certain someone in Seattle.

What really bothered her was this new development that left her packing her bags for Seattle. The planning must have been underway for months – it was certainly nothing Brandt could have pulled off in one weekend. Maybe he had intended for someone else to go. By now, there were others competent enough to do the job. The development had been a difficult and time-consuming process, but once the programming had been completed, the implementation was a breeze. Brandt must have recommended her at the last minute as a last-ditch effort to push her as far away from him as possible.

She fought her tears back. He had sent her away on a dinghy, and now she had to helplessly watch him walk down the plank. There was no lifesaver she could throw to him that he would accept. She could only hope and pray that he would stay afloat until he came to his senses, until he allowed his heart to be truly healed. She knew that she would be waiting for him still, if he ever found his way back to her.

City Limits

She arrived in Seattle that morning and was able to navigate to the address of her temporary residence without too much difficulty. She knocked on the door, nervously waiting to see who would greet her. Much to her relief, a young woman who appeared to be in her early twenties answered the door. She wore her dark brown hair in a short-bobbed style that was flipped out at the ends.

"You must be Ainsley. I'm Madison Gables, but everyone calls me Maddie," she greeted her. "Come on in." She graciously showed Ainsley to the room she would be sharing with Maddie. Ainsley quickly made the bed and started to unpack her suitcase. Instead of leaving Ainsley to get settled in, Maddie plopped down on her own bed to watch.

"So, how do you know Brandt?" she asked as Ainsley's heart stopped beating at the mention of his name.

"Brandt who?" she decided to play dumb. She wasn't sure who this Maddie was or how much she knew about her situation, but she wasn't about to reveal more than she had to.

"Brandt Cragun. You know – the guy who set you up with a place to stay?" Maddie sounded put out that she had to repeat herself.

"Oh, I work with him."

"So, you're LDS?"

"Why would you assume that?" Ainsley asked looking at the clothes she had just unpacked as if they were somehow evidence of her religion.

"Brandt mentioned it when he asked me about housing options. Lucky for you, Sarah's internship came through."

"Yeah, lucky me," Ainsley remarked sarcastically. "May I ask how you know him?"

"He's my cousin," Maddie explained. "And just between you and me, he's always been one of my favorites."

"I'm sure he has some endearing qualities once you get to know him," Ainsley stated, trying to distance herself from him as much as possible.

"He was never really the same after the divorce, or after the marriage, for that matter. I never did like his wife myself. No one did. He never saw her for what she was until it was too late," Maddie revealed. Ainsley tried not to act interested, but her curiosity won that short-lived tug-of-war. After all, she had heard Brady refer to Malissa in the same negative light, and this may be her only chance to hear the story Brandt wasn't willing to tell.

"What was so bad about her?"

"What wasn't would be the better question. She pursued Brandt after her fiancé broke up with her. They only dated for two weeks before they were engaged, and two months later they were married. His twin brother had just gotten married, and those two were pretty much inseparable. I think he was lonely and took the first thing that came along.

"She was a fake in every way and pulled the wool right over his eyes. I hoped for his sake I was wrong about her, but when she got pregnant right off, her true colors really came out. She wasn't the motherly type, and I think she resented Brandt and her daughter. I never saw her much after that, since she stopped coming to family functions. He tried to make it work for the sake of the kid. When her ex-fiancé came back into town a few years later, all of a sudden, she was aflutter with volunteer work four nights a week, only she wasn't volunteering anywhere but in her ex-fiancé's bedroom. The sad thing is that she's still the one who left him." Maddie certainly had no qualms about revealing the bones in Brandt's closet. Ainsley almost felt sorry for prying.

"That was probably too much personal information," Ainsley said uncomfortably. Brandt had never divulged much to her about his past or his ex-wife. She had hoped with time, he would come to trust her enough to share, but Brandt had severed that hope and sent her packing.

"I'm sorry. I probably shouldn't have said so much. Anyway, rumor has it he has a girlfriend in Portland. Maybe you can give me the juicy details," Maddie urged, excited by the prospect of more gossip to spread through the family tree. Ainsley's face suddenly became hot.

"He was dating someone," Ainsley confirmed, "but not anymore."

"That's too bad. What about you? Are you dating anyone?" Maddie prodded nosily.

"I was, but he conveniently broke up with me last weekend," Ainsley's voice cracked.

"Was it serious?" Maddie's blatant disregard for the fresh wounds Ainsley was trying to conceal was irritating, but Ainsley tried to be cordial.

"I thought so, but apparently, I was mistaken. I guess I was expecting more of a proposal than a disposal."

"In that case, you should totally come with me to the singles ward," she insisted.

"I don't think I'm up for that just yet."

"Okay, but really. You shouldn't pine away too long. We're not getting any younger after all," Maddie said as she left the room, much to Ainsley's relief.

"Thanks for the reminder," Ainsley muttered under her breath as she sat down on her bed. She was mulling over Brandt's relationship with his ex-wife, a relationship he did not relinquish willingly, despite her apparent infidelity. Ainsley contrasted that to his relationship with her. Although he had never told her that he loved her, she knew he had strong feelings for her. Why had he booted her out the door with no explanation when she had done nothing to hurt him? Her grief flared to life once again. She knew she needed to express her feelings to Brandt, so she could begin the process of letting go.

She pulled out a small box from her suitcase and opened it one last time. Inside she found the necklace Brandt had given her on her birthday. She ran her fingers over the smooth green heart-shaped glass that had once been volcanic ash. She abruptly closed the gates on the flood of memories that threatened to spill into her mind. Then, she pulled out a packet of fireweed seeds. She had intended to plant them in Brandt's yard as part of his birthday present, but those plans were no more. As she pulled out a piece of paper, her hand began to tremble. She took a deep breath to calm herself before penning a letter she wished she didn't have to write.

> *Dear Brandt,*
>
> *When Mt. St. Helens erupted, it seemed as if everything was destroyed. The fireweed plant was one of the first to start growing on the mountain again because its long roots reached through the ash to the soil underneath. I pray with all my*

heart that one day you will find your way to the soil again. Maybe these seeds can give you a little inspiration. I hope you have a happy birthday, and I'm sorry. I'm sorry for everything that has happened to you. I hope someday you find the happiness you deserve. Give Bridget a hug for me, and tell her I miss her! By the way, I'm re-gifting the birthday present you gave to me. It seems your heart crumbled after all, and you might be needing this one back.

~ Ainsley

She tucked the note inside the jewelry box and secured the seeds to it with a ribbon. Taking out another piece of paper, she addressed a letter to Bridget. Ainsley had finished the ribbon on the scrapbook Bridget made for her dad with the intention of mailing it to her in time for Brandt's birthday, although she doubted that Brandt would appreciate the fact that Ainsley was featured in several of the pictures Bridget had chosen to include. She regretted that she didn't have a chance to properly say goodbye to Bridget before she left, so she apologized in the letter and explained that she had to go out of town for a while for work.

She placed the jewelry box with the fireweed seeds along with Bridget's scrapbook in a box, ready to be mailed after work the following day. Her mother called that night to check in. Ainsley had called her on her way to Seattle, and she was disappointed to note the relief in her mother's voice when she found out Brandt had backed out of the relationship. She had never really come around to liking him, although Ainsley thought she had been making some headway with her mother.

"So, have you met any new friends yet, any guys?" her mom inquired, tossing any subtlety out the window. She didn't seem to understand how much Ainsley loved Brandt and Bridget.

"You know, Mom, I put up some wanted posters detailing what I was looking for in a man, but now that you mention it, I haven't had any responses. I'd better go check to see if someone took them down."

"Ainsley, don't be a smart aleck. I just worry about you," her mom retorted.

"Worry about never having grandkids, you mean. Don't you think it's hard enough for me without you hounding me about it?" Silence was the only response.

"Mom . . . are you still there?"

"I'm sorry, honey. I know you've been through a lot lately, but I still think it's for the best."

"Well, we'll have to agree to disagree on that point," Ainsley said before hanging up the phone in irritation.

The next two days, Ainsley woke up in just enough time to rush into work. When she came home, she went straight to her bedroom after eating a bowl of cold cereal for dinner. Her life seemed to be obscured by a fog that enveloped her every movement, sucking out all her motivation to do anything. On Thursday evening, Maddie barged into their shared bedroom unexpectedly.

"You're coming running with me in the morning," she announced.

"I'm what?" Ainsley rolled over to look at Maddie, her voice void of emotion.

"5:45. Hope you brought some running shoes."

"I don't run."

"You do now."

"Let me clarify: I don't run, and I don't intend to start now." Ainsley rolled back over and put the pillow over her head only to have Maddie pull it right back off.

"Listen. You've got to pull yourself together."

"What are you talking about? You don't even know me! Maybe this is my norm. Why don't you just buzz off?" Ainsley was getting perturbed.

"I seriously doubt you normally act like this, and besides, you've got a bad case of the break-up blues. Believe me, I've seen it before. Exercise with some new friends is just what the doctor ordered," Maddie persisted.

"Doctor smocter. Go away, and let me sleep," Ainsley said grumpily, and Maddie didn't press her any further. She walked out of the room, leaving Ainsley to drift off into a restless sleep. She was awakened at 5:30 the next morning by Maddie's one-woman band of pots and pans.

"Wake up, sleepy head, and lace up your shoes!" she instructed, far too cheerfully for the earliness of the hour. Ainsley ignored her.

"I'm not leaving until you get up," Maddie prodded while pulling Ainsley's covers off.

"Give me a break!" Ainsley growled groggily.

"Hurry up! Tori and Laithe are waiting." Ainsley rolled her eyes, but she knew there was no way Maddie was going to let her go back to sleep.

"I'll just be holding you up anyway," Ainsley reasoned.

"Nonsense! I've already told them you're a newbie."

"Okay. Okay," Ainsley admitted defeat as she dragged her legs over the side of her bed. Maddie tossed her some shoes and socks. In a few minutes, they were out the door.

Within blocks, Ainsley's side was throbbing, and she was sure her heart would explode from the exertion. If Maddie's friends were taking it slow, she was in some serious trouble. Ainsley pushed herself as hard as she could, but in the end, she had to walk the last half mile.

"Don't worry. We'll get you broken in," Maddie chimed from in front of her. Ainsley learned that Tori was Maddie's best friend. Maddie was attending college, finishing up her nursing degree, while Tori was a cosmetologist at an upscale Seattle salon. Laithe, who seemed to be completely infatuated with Tori, attended their singles ward, and he, too, was in college having recently returned from his mission. Ainsley felt like their grandmother as she shuffled behind them listening to their chatter about who liked whom in their ward.

Ainsley also discovered that Laithe had a roommate named Craig upon whom Maddie apparently had a huge crush. He usually ran with them as well, but he was picking up a good friend from the airport. His friend was from Germany, but he had served his mission in Seattle and baptized Craig's family five years ago. Ainsley didn't miss the singles ward scene one bit. Listening to their conversations only confirmed to her that she would definitely not be attending the singles ward with Maddie. She was going to try her luck with the home ward, hopefully blending into the background without being noticed.

Maddie woke her up at 5:30 on Saturday morning in her annoying jovial manner. Apparently, they ran Monday through Saturday, come rain or shine. Once again, Ainsley brought up the rear of the pack as she tried to keep up but found her body violently protesting with threats of imploding internal organs one by one. She reluctantly joined Maddie and Tori that evening for a girl's night out at a local restaurant.

"What am I going to do?" Tori complained. "I need a model for that makeover contest at work, and I can't find anyone who will agree to do it. I even tried to bribe a couple of my clients with free services, but they declined my very generous offer."

"I'd do it, but there's not much you can do to me that you haven't already done," Maddie admitted. Ainsley had been picking at her salad, only half listening to the conversation, when she realized that they were both staring at her.

121

"What?" Ainsley asked in alarm.

"What are you doing next Saturday, Ainsley?"

"Oh no! I'm not going to be your guinea pig," Ainsley protested.

"Come on. This is exactly what you need. There is no better way to get out of the dumps than by changing things up a little. New hairdo, new make-up, a few new outfits, and viola – you're a new person – new confidence, a fresh look, a fresh start…" Maddie tried to convince her.

"What exactly would this involve?" Ainsley found the idea somewhat intriguing.

"It would definitely involve cutting your hair, maybe some highlights…definitely a makeup overhaul and a wardrobe update. All free of charge, except the wardrobe update," Tori elaborated.

"Why not? What could it hurt?" Ainsley relented.

"Seriously?" Tori nearly jumped for joy.

"I'll agree if you follow a few simple rules. First, not too short. I don't want a pixie cut. Second, no crazy colors. I'm not going to walk into work with blue or green hair. Third, the hair that is cut must be donated to one of those foundations that makes wigs for cancer patients."

"You've got a deal! Tuesday we are going shopping after work."

Tori and Maddie dropped Ainsley by the apartment before heading off to a tri-stake singles dance, which Ainsley emphatically refused to attend. She was exhausted from her early morning and went to bed, which is where she had spent the majority of her first week in Seattle. Tomorrow, however, she would have to endure a church meeting as a new visitor, which would mean exchanging introductions and pleasantries. She would miss sitting by Deedra and Bridget, and of course Brandt, but there was no point dwelling on the past.

Ainsley entered the church building inconspicuously the following morning, settling onto a bench in the far corner of the chapel. She was reading the bulletin, trying to avoid contact with anyone, when she was interrupted by a deep, heavily accented male voice.

"Is anyone sitting here?" the voice belonged to a very handsome blonde man with piercing blue eyes who appeared to be about her age.

"Nope," she replied as cordially as she could.

"Do you mind if I do?"

"Not at all," she said as she put her scriptures under the bench.

"I'm new here – just visiting for a few weeks," he explained.

"Really? So am I," she answered in surprise.

"What brings you here?" he asked.

"Work. How about you?"

"I served my mission here and just came back to visit my good friends."

"Oh really? Where are you from?"

"Germany," he answered as the meeting got under way.

"You don't happen to be staying at Craig's apartment?" she asked, remembering her early morning run.

"Yes, I am. Do you know Craig?"

"No, actually I don't," she admitted. "I'm staying with one of his friends, Maddie Gables. I just heard her mention that he had a German friend coming to stay with him."

"Ah, Maddie, yes. Craig talks about Maddie quite frequently," he laughed.

"What brings you to the home ward? I thought you'd be going to the singles ward with Craig and Laithe?" she probed.

"I served in this ward for several months. It was a home away from home for a while, so I wanted to attend here," he said as the meeting got underway.

As sacrament meeting adjourned, he shook her hand, smiling as he said,

"Hope to see you around." Ainsley hurried off to Relief Society, where an older woman sat next to her.

"Are you new in the ward?" she asked.

"Not permanently. I'm here for six weeks for work."

"Oh, I see. Where are you from?"

"Portland, Oregon," Ainsley answered.

"Two of my children live in Portland and a bunch of my grandkids."

"Really? It's a small world. Portland is a great place to live for the most part."

"I'm Betty, by the way," the woman introduced herself.

"I'm Ainsley. Nice to meet you." Ainsley was relieved when a woman stood at the front of the room to start relief society, so she didn't have to engage in anymore small talk. She slipped out of the building as soon as the meeting was over. *One Sunday down, five to go*, she thought as she drove back to the apartment.

The next morning, she was awakened by Maddie again for her prescribed treatment of running. Ainsley was surprised to see the blonde man from church waiting outside with the rest of the group. She was embarrassed that she hadn't asked his name, and even more embarrassed that she was going to humiliate herself in front of him with her huffing and puffing and frequent rest stops.

"This is my temporary roommate, Ainsley Nelson," Maddie introduced her.

"This is Craig Williams, and his friend, Dietrich Krause, who's visiting from Germany."

"We've met," Ainsley said.

"At church yesterday," she added as she noticed the inquiring looks. Turning to Dietrich, she apologized, "Sorry I never asked for your name." The others started their slow-paced run for Ainsley's sake.

"No problem," he replied.

"Just so you know, I'm new to this whole running thing, so you probably

124

don't want to run by me. I'll just slow you down. And a word of caution, I should have one of those signs posted on me that warns people behind me that this vehicle makes frequent stops."

"A small price to pay for good company," he responded as he settled into her slow pace. She found herself blushing at his comment, which was a refreshing change for her. Dietrich joined them on their morning runs, and Ainsley looked forward to their little chats. He was a fascinating individual with so many stories to tell, and she enjoyed being in his company.

On Tuesday evening, Tori was true to her word and met Ainsley at the door when she came home from work. They shopped until Ainsley thought she might drop dead if she had to try on one more outfit. Deedra would definitely get along well with Tori. She had never met anyone who equaled Deedra in her love for shopping until she spent the evening with Tori. Luckily for her, Tori was all about value shopping, while the price tag on an item meant little to Deedra. When all was said and done, Ainsley came home with five new outfits, and three new dresses including a black party dress, which she was supposed to wear for her big reveal the evening of the makeover.

Saturday arrived before Ainsley had fully mentally prepared herself for it. After the morning run, she showered, and Tori picked her up for the all-day event. Tori's only rule was that Ainsley wouldn't be allowed to see herself until just before she was escorted on stage. Ainsley nearly cried when she felt the weight of her hair disappear with a few snips of Tori's scissors. She imagined that it must be only a small degree of what cancer victims felt when their hair fell out in clumps against their will. That offered more than enough consolation for Ainsley to pull herself together. She was primped and poked, washed and waxed, and swiveled and swirled around until she thought she was going to be dizzy from the flurry of activity about her. Finally, Tori was done. She brought out a full-sized mirror, and Ainsley was nearly stunned to death as she stared at the stranger's reflection that peered back at her.

"So? Do you like?" Tori asked anxiously.

"Who is she?" Ainsley answered, touching her face to make sure she was staring at her own reflection. Her hair was cut in a short A-line bob. The underneath was colored a deep brown and varying colors of highlights were woven throughout the top.

"You don't like it?" Tori's face sagged with disappointment.

"Like it? I love it. I look like a supermodel, but without the sunken cheeks, crazy hair, and heavy makeup. It's awesome!" Tori let out a squeal of delight.

"We are so going to win this," she predicted, and so it was. Victoria "Tori" Harris was declared the winner, and her salon was presented with a prestigious award and a cover spot on a popular hair magazine, which also meant that Ainsley's face was plastered all over the cover as well. It was all so disconcerting, but Ainsley came to like the attention. She found a new confidence that had been dormant her entire life.

That night everyone went out to celebrate at a nice restaurant that offered dinner and dancing. Of course, Craig and Maddie paired off, Laithe and Tori paired off, and Ainsley found herself sitting alone at the table with Dietrich. He leaned over and said something to her, but she didn't understand what he was saying. When she asked him to repeat himself, he said, "You probably can't understand me through my accent."

"I've always been more drawn to the British accent myself," she quipped.

"British, ha!" he said pretending to be offended. "That's a girly accent. You need a German accent, manly, gruff, yet eloquent enough to woo the ladies."

"I always thought the Italians were the amorous ones, or is it the French? At any rate, I was wrong. It seems the Germans beat the Italians and the French hands down."

"The new look is very nice by the way," Dietrich refocused the conversation. "You're very beautiful, both before and after." She blushed as he spoke.

"I just have to wonder why you aren't married," he probed.

Here we go again, she thought.

"Honestly, Dietrich, the opportunity has never presented itself. I guess I'm ever the buddy never the bride."

"I don't understand these American men," he said shaking his head in bafflement.

"That makes two of us," she agreed. Who needed Ben and Jerry when she had Dietrich?

"What about you? Why haven't you tied the knot yet?"

"Certainly not from the lack of looking. Good LDS girls are hard to find in my small town in Germany."

"That's a good enough excuse, I guess."

"Would you care to dance?" he asked. The last time she had danced was on her birthday when Brandt had taken her ballroom dancing. The memory threatened to disrupt the revelry of the evening. Dietrich sensed her hesitation and didn't wait for a response. He simply grabbed her hand and escorted her to the dance floor. She did not find him lacking as her dance partner.

"I wasn't going to take no for an answer," he whispered in her ear before twirling her around. She had a pleasant evening in the company of Dietrich, but she couldn't help feeling like a traitor to Bridget and even to Brandt. Not only that, but she felt as if she were betraying herself, enjoying a burst of happiness when everything inside her was just now tingling with sadness after the numbness that had nested in her heart.

The next morning, which happened to be Sunday, she was sitting by

Dietrich when she saw the woman, who had introduced herself as Betty in relief society the previous Sunday, enter the chapel. Ainsley's pulse quickened as she saw Brandt's face appear in the doorway, following Betty. He had come looking for her, to apologize. Her hope was quickly drowned by the anchor of reality when she saw Eve behind him with their six children. It was only Brady after all. Ainsley wasn't sure if she should talk to them or not. She wasn't even sure they would recognize her with her new look.

As she was silently debating with herself, she saw Eve turn her head, glancing around the chapel for familiar faces. At first, she looked right past Ainsley but quickly did a double take. Eve bumped Brady in the arm to get his attention and leaned close to whisper something in his ear. He turned around, all subtlety abandoned as usual, fixing his eyes in Ainsley's direction. It was so disarming to see him because it was like seeing Brandt all over again, an image she was trying to erase. Brady branded his face with a big smile and gave her a thumbs up. Ainsley blushed, and Eve knocked the back of Brady's head in dismay.

"Someone you know?" Dietrich leaned over to ask as the meeting started.

"A family I know from Portland," she said. "They must be visiting relatives."

As soon as the meeting ended, Eve rushed over to say hello. Ainsley hadn't spoken to Brady or Eve after Brandt broke up with her. She felt more than a little awkward. Eve hugged Ainsley.

"It's so good to see you again. We heard you were in Seattle for work but never thought in a million years we'd bump into you. And just look at you! I hardly recognized you with your haircut," she said as the rest of the family filed into the pew behind her.

"It's a small world it seems," Ainsley responded. "What brings you here?"

"Oh, the daughter of a close friend was baptized yesterday. We decided to stay with Brady's parents instead of driving back last night. Have you met them yet?" she asked, ushering Betty to her side.

"Briefly," Ainsley smiled at the older woman, "but I never caught her last name." Betty seemed confused at the entire exchange.

"Am I missing something?" she asked.

"Mom," Brady interjected, "this is Ainsley Nelson."

"Yes, yes," she said still bewildered, "I met her last Sunday, but how do you know her?" There was a bit of awkward silence. What exactly was she? She couldn't really be introduced as Brandt's ex-girlfriend, maybe a colleague or his next-door neighbor, and then she had a brilliant idea that bypassed her relationship with Brandt altogether.

"I am Bridget's activity day leader," she announced, "and I also happen to live next door to her."

"Oh," Betty Cragun's face flushed with sudden insight. Apparently, someone had enlightened her on Brandt's recent escapades.

"It's so good to finally meet you. Bridget speaks very highly of you," Betty Cragun said. Dietrich cleared his throat as people began filling the chapel for Sunday School. Betty escorted her grandchildren to Primary as Brady looked from Ainsley to Dietrich and back to Ainsley again.

"And who is this dashing young fellow?" he asked.

"Oh. I'm sorry," she said. "This is Dietrich Krause." Dietrich shook Brady's extended hand.

"Krause?" he repeated. "Is that German?"

"Yes, I am visiting from Germany," Dietrich answered, his accent verifying his origins. With that, Brady launched into German, apparently asking Dietrich a question because Dietrich answered in German.

Eve turned to Ainsley with an explanation, "Brady served his mission in

Germany and is always eager to talk to someone in German, so his language skills don't get rusty. I'll never get him to shut up now."

"It looks like they're ready to start," Ainsley noted while taking a seat. Eve sat beside her, pulling Brady with her, and Dietrich sat down next to Brady. When Betty finally returned, the only space left was on Ainsley's other side.

"I'd be happy to move if your husband needs a seat," she whispered to Betty.

"Not necessary. Frank teaches the sixteen-year-old Sunday school class," she explained as she patted Ainsley's arm. Ainsley found herself surrounded by Cragun's once again. There was no escaping them no matter which fork in the road of choices she took or was forced to take in this case. She always seemed to be bumping into one of them as though her auto-pilot was set on a Cragun collision course. As the lesson got underway, Eve leaned toward Ainsley.

"Listen," she whispered, "I know what happened between you and Brandt."

"At least that makes one of us," Ainsley interjected. "I'm curious as to what exactly he told you happened."

"To be honest, he's been pretty tight-lipped. He told us that it wasn't going to work out between the two of you, but we can all read between the lines. We know there's more to the story than that. Eventually, Brady will find out what's going on, if it doesn't kill him first. I'm not even sure if Brandt knows himself. We are all heartbroken because you're like a part of the family. Hey, why don't you come over for dinner tonight for old times' sake?" Eve suggested, which is how Ainsley found herself eating dinner at Frank and Betty Cragun's house that evening.

Surprisingly, Ainsley felt comfortable as though this was just a big family dinner party she was invited to every Sunday. Brady's parents were amiable, funny, and welcoming, and dinner flew by with light conversation that never once turned to the subject of Brandt. Ainsley received an update on Bridget from the twins, who went on and on about how Bridget was going to be so jealous that they got to eat Sunday dinner with her. Ainsley realized just how much she had missed all of them, Bridget in particular.

Ainsley was helping with the dinner dishes in the kitchen when she saw a drawing prominently displayed on the refrigerator. She could tell immediately that Bridget was the artist. The drawing featured a small family of three. A little girl with blonde bouncy curls claimed the center of the drawing. On one side, she was holding hands with a man she had labeled dad. On the other side she was holding hands with a long, blonde-haired woman she had labeled Zee. Tears welled up in Ainsley's eyes, and she wanted to reach out to tear herself out of the picture just as Brandt had done.

"Ainsley?" Eve had been talking to her, but she hadn't heard a word she had said. Eve walked to where Ainsley was standing and glanced at the drawing.

Ainsley quickly blinked her tears away, saying, "You know, I just remembered I have to go. . . I have something. . . I mean. . . I have to meet someone. . . I mean call someone. I just have to go. Thanks a lot for dinner. It was delicious. Sorry. . . I shouldn't have come..." She was out the front door before anyone could protest.

She drove without a destination in mind. It wasn't until she parked her car and began to walk that she realized where she had gone. She was at the edge of the pond where Brandt had first held her hand. If she was trying to get her mind off him, she wasn't doing a very good job of it. She didn't try to stop the memories from coming, instead she embraced them. She closed her eyes and relived every second she had spent with him. It was the little things she missed the most: the sound of Bridget's laugh, the touch of Brandt's hand in hers, and even the smell of his deodorant. Once or twice, she had caught herself wandering down the deodorant aisle to catch a whiff of his Old Spice, just to remember him.

She wanted so badly to hate him, but she couldn't force herself to do it. Even when her mind was filled with the first months of him acting like Mr. Road Rage, she couldn't conjure up an ounce of hate. Instead, she re-lived those moments from a different perspective: his insults became gentle teasing, and his icy glares melted into pools of sadness. She cried. The tears ran down her cheeks like rain, acid rain, searing her soul into smoldering pieces with each drop.

The next morning, Maddie stood over her bed with a squirt bottle, threatening to spray if she didn't get up. Ainsley reluctantly pulled herself out of her short slumber. She hadn't come home until after midnight, but her early morning wake-up party was waiting, Dietrich included.

"Rough night?" he asked as they jogged.

"You know those people you met at church yesterday?"

"Yeah, really nice guy, that Brady."

"Well, Brady is the twin brother of my ex-boyfriend. They invited me over for dinner for old times' sake, and like an idiot I went. I thought I could handle it, but...well...let's just say, it was stupid of me. I didn't handle it so well. I ended up leaving abruptly," she confessed, and she was relieved to finally talk to someone about it who wasn't tainted by bias like her mother.

"How long ago did you break up?"

"Two weeks ago."

"Wow. You're not even on the rebound yet. That's not even enough time for reality to sink in."

"You've been down this road before, I take it."

"It was about six months ago. I thought I'd met the love of my life, and I guess she didn't quite see it that way."

"How did you get over it?"

"I'll let you know when I find out."

"What kind of encouragement is that?" She hit him playfully in the arm.

"The honest kind."

"I see. I've got a long road ahead of me, then."

"It's easier if you have someone to talk through it with. What do you say we go out to dinner tonight?"

"I do believe I'll take you up on that offer. If I have to be around the lovebirds tonight, I think I might just go nuts myself."

Dietrich was right; it was nice to be around someone who knew what she was going through. She found herself spending more and more time with Dietrich over the next few weeks. She even began to look forward to running every morning, and shockingly, her body wasn't protesting as loudly as it had before. Maddie made sure that her evenings were filled with activities ranging from Wii tournaments to Halloween parties, all of which included Dietrich as well. Maddie was clearly trying her hand at matchmaking, and Ainsley wasn't quite sure how she felt about that. She wasn't ready to move past Brandt until she found out exactly why everything had fallen apart so abruptly. That prompted a blunt conversation with Maddie one afternoon. A conversation that Ainsley had been putting off since she first found out that Maddie was Brandt's cousin.

"Maddie, I have a confession to make," Ainsley began.

"Oh, do tell," Maddie was always salivating for a fresh piece of gossip.

"I am the girl Brandt was dating," she finally admitted.

"Brandt is Mr. Disposal?" she questioned in disbelief.

"I'm afraid so."

"What the heck happened between you two?"

"I wish I knew. Apparently, he hasn't told anyone what the problem is. All

I know is that he disappeared to come to Seattle for a weekend, and nobody knows why. When he came back, and I'm talking like the minute he got back, he gave me the typical it's-not-going-to-work-out-between-us spill with no other explanation at all, other than the reassurance that leaving me was the best for both of us. That Monday I showed up at work to find out I was being transferred for six weeks at Brandt's recommendation."

"How convenient for him. Is he your boss or something?"

"No. We don't even work in the same department, but he has a powerful influence over the head honcho of financial services apparently, if he's calling in personal favors that aren't necessarily in the best interest of the grants department."

"Wow. I never would have pegged him as one to do that."

"Neither would I, and I never would have believed he was capable of it if I hadn't been on the receiving end."

"So, what about Dietrich?"

"What about Dietrich? It's not like I haven't told him more than once that I'm still trying to get over a serious relationship that I didn't want to end. Besides, he's still nursing a broken heart too."

"Well, Craig seems to think that the only reason Dietrich is still around is because of you. He only planned on staying here for two weeks, and he's been here almost six. Apparently, you're just what the doctor ordered for his broken heart, and I'm guessing he's thinking he's your best medicine too."

"Dietrich is one of the nicest guys I know, but I'm not about to rush into a relationship that I'm not ready to commit to. Every minute I spend with him I feel like a turncoat. The name Benedict Arnold keeps popping into my head. I feel like I'm letting Brandt down, even though he doesn't want anything to do with me. I don't know what I'm supposed to do. I keep hoping Brandt will come to his senses, and at least talk to me about whatever happened, but I haven't heard anything from him since I left. It's as if he simply erased me. Out of sight, out of mind. I like Dietrich, I do, but I love Brandt."

"Wow," Maddie seemed to be speechless for the first time since Ainsley had met her.

"What? No words of wisdom for me?"

"I'd say you're stuck between a rock and a hard place, and I'll be interested to see what comes of it all."

"Gee, thanks a lot."

"Ainsley, have you considered how long you plan to pine away over Brandt?"

"Well...I guess...well..." Ainsley stopped to consider her answer for a moment. "I guess I convinced myself we were just in hiatus. I'll quit pining when I can convince myself it's really over, and this just isn't a bad nightmare from which I can't seem to wake up. I suppose that will happen sooner than later since my little vacation is ending, and I'll have to deal with seeing him every day. That will be the true test."

Indeed, her time in Seattle was drawing to a close. She had only one week left. The weather had turned cold as mid-November approached, and Ainsley found herself dreading her return to Portland. On Tuesday evening, Dietrich had invited her to go to a movie with him. They were waiting for it to start when she asked, "How long are you here for anyway?"

"I just bought a one-way ticket. I wasn't sure how long I'd want to stay," he smiled at her with his broad, perfect smile, and she wanted to hide behind it to ward off the sadness and confusion that seemed to sneak up on her these days.

"Don't you have to get back for work or something?"

"No, I work for my father. Right now, I'm telecommuting halfway across the world. He doesn't care where I am as long as I get done what needs to be done."

"That's convenient."

"Very," he said as the lights dimmed and the movie previews began to play.

After the movie, they went for a walk in a nearby park. There was a chill in the air, but the rain had subsided for the moment. Ainsley tripped on a slick, uneven section of the sidewalk as they were walking. Dietrich grabbed her hand to steady her but never let go. Ainsley wasn't sure what to do, so she just kept walking with her hand entwined in his. They stopped at a park bench and sat down, even though it was still wet. He leaned in to kiss her, but she stopped him, taking his face in her hands. He opened his eyes, surprised.

"Dietrich," she said, "I think you are a really great guy, and if we had met a few months ago, things might have worked out differently between us. But I'm not going to string you along when I can't love you like you want me too. Not right now, anyway. My heart hasn't healed yet, and when I look into your eyes, you're perfectly blue eyes that are so opposite his, I can only see him. No matter how hard I try, no matter how much I want him to go away, his image always masks your face. It's not fair to you." She started to cry – tears for hurting Dietrich, tears of self-pity, tears of heartbreak. Dietrich gathered her up in his arms, hugging her close to him and stroking her hair, while speaking soft words of consolation in German. He held her as she cried. When the crying abated, he lifted her head and looked into her eyes as he wiped her tears with his hand.

"Do not be sorry for me. I am sure there is someone out there for me, and when I'm ready, I will find her, or she will find me. Even I have to admit, the odds weren't in our favor, but it was fun while it lasted, yeah?" She smiled as he spoke.

"But for you, Ainsley, I will pray. I will pray that your heart can be healed. I will pray that this man realizes what he has lost and comes for you again - only because that is what you want, not because he deserves it." He then leaned forward and pressed his lips against hers, and this time she didn't resist. She kissed him back in gratitude for his friendship and kindness. When he withdrew, his eyes were twinkling, and his smile was broader than she had ever seen it.

"Thank you," he said as he stood up, offering her his arm. She took it, and they walked arm in arm to her car. When she dropped him off, he turned to her before opening his door.

"This is goodbye. I think my time here has drawn to a close. Tomorrow I shall see if I can't catch a plane home. I wish you the best," he said as he got out of the car.

"Goodbye," she whispered as she watched him disappear in the shadows.

"Best of luck to you too," she called after him.

Her heart felt like a crumpled piece of paper that had been wadded carelessly into a ball, and now she was left to smooth out all the wrinkles without ripping its delicate fibers to pieces. Friday arrived before she knew it. She had reached Seattle's city limits, and it was time to finally face her own Goliaths back in Portland. She only hoped she could fend them off as well as little Kellan had.

Homeward Bound

Ainsley had her bags pretty much packed and ready to go when Maddie opened the door to their room.

"You're not leaving tonight, you know," she said nonchalantly.

"Oh, really?"

"We're having a farewell party for you tonight."

"Well," Ainsley paused to reconsider. "Why hasten the execution, right?"

"I wish you didn't have to go just yet."

"I may be back sooner than later. I heard some of the employees talking at work that a permanent position was going to be opening up after the new year, and I'm seriously thinking about applying for it. I just can't picture myself staying in Portland after all that has happened there, you know?"

"You'll always have a welcome reception here," Maddie said as they headed out the door.

The next morning, after one last run with Maddie and her gang, Ainsley was settling into the driver's seat of her car to go home when her phone rang.

"Hey, Mom. What's up?" There was no response, and Ainsley could hear sniffling in the background.

"Mom? Is everything okay? Where are you?'

"It's your dad, honey. He's had a heart attack," her mom barely choked the words out before she burst into tears again.

"I'll be right there," she said. She was headed home after all, just not the home she had intended. As she drove, she realized that life was just like a road filled with potholes, unexpected curves and switchbacks, and even the occasional sinkhole. Some potholes were easy to steer clear of for her – the potholes of addiction or immorality. Others, she didn't even see until the car had already driven into them – the potholes of betrayal or unexpected illness. Then, there were the times when she felt confident in the direction her life was going only to encounter an unforeseen switchback that sent her in the opposite direction, slowing her progress and testing her faith. Right now, she envisioned herself on a switchback filled with potholes she couldn't seem to navigate no matter which way she veered her vehicle. She just hoped that a sinkhole wasn't on the horizon. Fourteen agonizing hours later, Ainsley pulled into the Logan Regional Hospital parking lot. She rushed to the waiting room where she found her mother dozing off in a chair.

"Mom," Ainsley whispered, gently patting her mom's arm. Her mom opened her eyes and then contorted her face in an expression of horror.

Ainsley's hand shot to her hair. It was only then that she remembered she had purposely failed to mention her makeover. Her mother was very fond of her long hair, and this must have been a terrible shock, especially after all that had happened today.

"I'm sorry, Mom. Did I forget to mention that I cut my hair? How's Dad?" Her mother took her time gathering her thoughts before she finally responded.

"He's going to pull through. The nurse just gave me an update about twenty minutes ago that the surgery is going well. He had to have four bypasses, but they think he has an excellent chance of making a full recovery," she explained.

"That's so good to hear. I've been worried sick the whole drive," Ainsley sat back in the chair and took a long, deep breath.

"What on earth have you done to yourself? What happened to all your beautiful, beautiful hair?" Thus began a long lecture about how Brandt was the source of all the negative things in her life, and he was to blame for her drastic makeover, which her mother added, made her look as if she were trying to blend in with the scoffers from the great and spacious building. Ainsley had long since stopped arguing with her mother. She sat back in her chair and closed her eyes, ignoring the long discourse as best she could.

Her father was in the hospital for a week and a half. Ainsley requested the rest of her vacation days so she could help her mother, and Jed Corbett was more than obliging after he heard that there was a family emergency. Because she had only taken a few days here and there for vacation to go to the beach and to Silver Falls with Brandt and Bridget that summer, she still had nearly three weeks left, which she had to use before the end of the year anyway.

She realized as she walked in the front door of her parent's home that she hadn't been there in over a year. She felt a tinge of regret and guilt at having stayed away so long. She avoided coming home around major holidays like she avoided the plague, particularly Thanksgiving and Christmas. She usually convinced her parents to fly or drive to Oregon for a visit instead. The few times she had come home over the last six years, she inevitably ran into one of her classmates from high school with his or her family in tow, and awkward conversations ensued. She tired of constantly being asked if she was dating anyone or if she had put marriage off in order to pursue a career. Visits home wore on her nerves.

Ainsley settled into a routine rather quickly, although she was overwhelmed with all the kindness the ward members exhibited. The freezer was packed with food well-wishers had dropped by. She was ever grateful to Maddie for making her run because she found her 5:30 jaunt not only invigorating, but also her one source of solace from the chaos that seemed to be surrounding her. Her mother was trying to be less overbearing with the exception of the Samson analogies she kept slipping in every now and again after her first lecture about Ainsley's makeover.

What surprised Ainsley more than anything was how her father's brush with death had transformed him. He was much more sentimental than he had been before. Ainsley had never had a really good heart-to-heart talk with her dad, but now he seemed willing to listen to the unfiltered and uncensored version of the events that had recently transpired in her life, her mother being the filter and censor. He listened with a sympathetic ear and offered her the encouragement and approval her mother withheld. She was grateful to have a second chance with him.

Two weeks into her stay her mother sauntered into the living room after helping her dad get settled in for an afternoon nap. "Honey, I have some good news for you," she said.

"Oh?"

"I arranged for you to get out of the house tomorrow night," she announced.

"What are you talking about?"

"Rupert Allen dropped by to see how your father was while you were at the grocery store this morning. I thought it might be a nice change for you if you went out to dinner with him tomorrow," she said as casually as if she had arranged for a surprise spa appointment, expecting Ainsley to gush with gratitude.

"Rupert Allen? Mom!" Ainsley was horrified that her mother would sink so low.

"He's a nice young man –"

"Young?" Ainsley shrieked. "He was young a hundred years ago!" Rupert Allen had to be pushing 50, at least.

"Honey, you need to get out. You've been cooped up in the house since you came," her mom said defensively, although it sounded more like pleading.

"Mom, I came home to help you with Dad, not to be set up with any available bachelor in Franklin. Rupert Allen? I cannot believe you! This has to be ranked among the unpardonable sins that mothers can commit against their daughters," Ainsley was exasperated by her mother's encroachment into her personal life. To set her up with someone like Rupert Allen was more than Ainsley could bear at the moment.

"Well, he'd never treat you like that Brandt character did, and you're not walking into a ready-made family." Her mom never knew when it was time to give up. She always had to give a little extra shove that sent Ainsley tumbling over her cliff of fury. Ainsley's rage manifested itself as a pooling of tears in her eyes, but she was determined not to let one drop slip. Her mom had never warmed up to the idea of Ainsley dating Brandt.

"Mom, you never gave him a chance. Don't talk to me about things you don't know anything about."

"I do understand one thing: he broke your heart," her mom stated emphatically.

"But what you don't understand is that I'd rather live with a broken heart and be all alone for the rest of my life than trade all the happiness and love I felt for those five months. I'll take that pleasure for this pain, if that's the price I have to pay to have felt so alive and so in love. I'd rather have that than a loveless marriage to someone like Rupert Allen, who would probably leave me widowed by the time I was 40 anyway," her mom sat in shocked disbelief at Ainsley's backlash. She had never considered how much Ainsley had loved Brandt. She just figured it was a little fling.

"And another thing," Ainsley continued, "I love Bridget just as much as I imagine I would love her if she were my own flesh and blood. So, you're right... I was walking into a ready-made family – one that God had custom built just for me. Mom, I don't understand why events unfolded as they did, but I have faith that God is guiding my life. I've felt it. What others dismiss as coincidences or accidents, I see as God's hand directing the traffic in my life, and He's never steered me wrong. Now, I just have to be patient and let Him do what needs to be done, and one day I'll be able to look back at this little dark spot in my life only to find that it was never dark at all. I was just looking out the window with the shades drawn." Ainsley spoke the answer to her own prayers.

She heard the words in her own familiar voice, but they were words she had never thought before. She felt peace rush over her like a soft, refreshing breeze as she walked out of the kitchen and into her bedroom. Whether she and Brandt were meant to be together, she did not know. Whether her heart would ever fully recover, she did not know. Whether her permanent relocation to Seattle would actually take place, she did not know. However, she did know now with absolute certainty that everything would work out in the end.

An hour later, her mom knocked softly on her door. She didn't wait for an invitation from her daughter before she walked in. Ainsley could tell that her mom's eyes were puffy and red from crying. She sat down on the bed next to Ainsley, handing her a large manila envelope from Deedra.

"This came for you in the mail," her mom said, but as Ainsley began to open it, her mom reached out to stop her. "Wait. Before you open it, I want to show you what I got in the mail."

She held out another envelope. It was a card from Bridget addressed specifically to Ainsley's mom and dad. Bridget had drawn a large heart. Inside the heart, she had drawn a girl with bouncy blonde curls praying by her bedside. Inside the card Bridget had written that every day she prayed for Ainsley's dad to get better and for Ainsley's mom to be comforted. She wrote that she hoped to one day meet both of them, maybe during an Idaho winter so she could see a real blizzard. She ended with, "I love you even though I don't know you." As usual, God's timing was impeccable. Ainsley looked up at her mom, who was crying again.

"She's a special little girl. I'm sorry I've been so... hypocritical and judgmental and pushy. I wondered why Heavenly Father wasn't answering my prayers for you, but I see now that he was – just not in the way I wanted. I called Rupert to cancel the date for tomorrow. I'm sorry, honey. I'm so sorry," she gave her daughter a hug and left the room.

Ainsley opened the envelope to find cards from her activity day girls inside. Deedra had enclosed a letter explaining that Bridget hijacked the last activity day, urging everyone to make cards for Ainsley to cheer her up. Ainsley smiled at all the sentiments and pictures, comforted by the thought that she was missed.

When she checked her e-mail later that evening, she was surprised to see a message from Dietrich. She hadn't heard from him since his return to Germany. She clicked on the message and read:

Ainsley,

I hope you don't mind me sending you a short e-mail. At least I felt like we parted as good friends, and I'd like to keep it that way. I enjoyed our time together in Seattle, and I want you to know how much I admire your loyalty. I also wanted to tell you that I met someone in the most miraculous way that it is impossible for me to deny God's hand in it. I caught a plane back to Germany early the morning following our last night together. There was only one flight out that day that wasn't already booked, and I got the last remaining seat, so I was unable to choose my seat location. A German woman named Jana (pronounced Yana) sat next to me. I decided to strike up a conversation with her. You can imagine my surprise when I found out that she had recently graduated from an American university and was returning to Germany to start a new job in a city very near my hometown. She noticed my CTR ring and told me that she was a member of the church too. I offered my services as a tour guide, and well, I guess as they say, the rest is history. I cringe to think if I hadn't left when I did that our paths may have never crossed. You see, I had no intention of leaving Seattle so suddenly if not for you. Ainsley, God directs our lives. He directed mine through you, and I know all things will work out for your good too.

Your friend always,
Dietrich

Ainsley wrote Dietrich an e-mail of congratulations and thanked him for his friendship. She wiped a tear from her eye as she typed. She was grateful that someone had finally found happiness, and Dietrich was a deserving recipient if there ever was one.

Her father was on the road to recovery when she bid farewell a week later. She knew the ward members would take good care of her parents in her absence, which offered her consolation on her long trip back. When she pulled into her own driveway twelve hours later, her stomach sank when she saw the lights on in Brandt's house. She felt like a stranger in a familiar land clouded by the haze of absence. She had half expected time to stand still in Portland while she was gone, but it had trudged ahead without her.

There was no evidence that the trees had once donned leaves in every hue because they had been laid to rest in dumpsters and compost piles concealed from view. There was no evidence that a burglar had once broken the front window of her house aside from the bright blue sign posted prominently on the lawn indicating that the house was now protected by an alarm system. There was no evidence that the house next door had once been the birthplace of her love. There was no welcoming party to greet her. Even for a Sunday night, all was too silent. Life had moved on without her; the thought tightened the knot that had formed in her stomach upon her arrival, threatening to squeeze to death the small shred of courage to face the days ahead that she had managed to create. Only two months and one week had passed, but it felt like years had snuck by. *Was it all just a dream after all?* she thought to herself.

Grafting Hearts

"I'm so glad you're back, Zee!" Bridget exclaimed. "I've missed you. Deedra isn't much of an activity day leader without you." Bridget had burst through her door not too long after she came home from work, which was around 7:00 that Monday night. Ainsley had a lot of catching up to do and was happy to occupy her spare time at work since she had nothing better to do. The further away she was from Brandt, the stronger she felt.

"Thanks, Bridget," Ainsley smiled, "but you know I'm not sure how much longer I'll be able to stay here." She didn't want to give Bridget any false hope, since life wasn't going to go back to how it used to be.

"Why?" Bridget frowned as she plopped herself on the couch.

"As soon as a job opens up, I'm most likely moving to Seattle," Ainsley answered honestly.

"I hate Seattle," Bridget said grumpily. "Seattle is nothing but bad luck."

Ainsley did not want to have this conversation.

"I don't know how it feels to go through all that you've been through, but it must be hard for you. I imagine it really stinks, but I can't stay here. I promise to drop by to see you whenever I visit Deedra though. We'll set up a girl's night out every month," she tried to explain. She gave Bridget a hug, but Bridget burst into tears.

"I didn't mean to make you cry, Bridge," Ainsley said, wiping Bridget's tears away with her shirt sleeve.

"Please don't go," Bridget pleaded through her tears. "I need you here. Nothing has been the same since you left. I overheard my dad talking to my Uncle Brady a couple of weeks ago. He said my mom was trying to take me away from him to live with her in Seattle, so I could help out with her new baby. I bet you didn't know she had a baby, did you?" Ainsley shook her head, and her heart sank like a boulder inside her chest.

"Oh, Bridget," she comforted, "I'm so sorry."

"I knew something was going on, but my dad never said anything about it. He didn't want anyone to know, so that's why he said he had to take that work trip to Seattle," Ainsley was anxious to hear the rest of the story. "He met my mom to try to talk her out of it. He didn't want me to have to go through a custody battle." These were burdens a ten-year-old should never have to bear, being thrust into an adult world – into a war really – torn between two sides, straddling a fault line caused by the earthquake of divorce. Bridget was still suffering aftershocks three years later. Ainsley stroked Bridget's blonde hair, feeling a tear trickle down her cheek as well.

"He told Uncle Brady that he convinced her not to fight for permanent custody. It's not like she's had anything to do with me since she left anyway. All she wants is a servant now that she's strapped down with another kid. So, I don't have to live with her, but I have to spend Christmas vacation with her and six weeks in the summer. I have to leave on Thursday, and I don't want to go!"

"Bridget, have you talked to your dad about this?" Ainsley was searching for the right words to say.

"He just told me last night officially, although I already knew. He used his typical line that it would be for the best and that she was still my mom, so I need to give her a chance," Bridget replied.

"You know sometimes we don't understand why certain things happen to us, and life just doesn't seem fair. But do you know what I've learned? God knows you, and He knows what's going on. He loves you very, very much – more than you can ever know, and if you ask Him, He will help you through this, and He'll help you become a better person because of it, if you let Him."

"But I don't think my mom even goes to church anymore," she countered.

"Well . . . there's an opportunity then. Maybe He wants you to be an example for her and your new brother or sister."

"It's a brother. Keenan is his name," she told her.

"See. . . Keenan needs you, and you'll get some great babysitting experience. There's good money to be made in babysitting these days. Besides, I bet you could go to church with your grandparents if you wanted to," she said. Bridget smiled. Her crying subsided, and she seemed consoled, at least for now.

"May I offer a little friendly advice for the future? I wouldn't recommend listening in on anymore of your dad's conversations," Bridget laughed with Ainsley, as Ainsley added, "Who knows – maybe we'll meet up in Seattle next summer."

Bridget gave her a hug and said, "Thanks, Zee. I've missed you so much. I don't really understand what happened between my dad and you, but I liked him a lot better when you were around. He hasn't been the same since you left either." Ainsley didn't understand why Brandt couldn't have told her what was happening, and she didn't understand why a custody battle would prompt him to turn his back on her.

Despite the cold temperatures and rain, she kept to her routine of running early every morning. On Tuesday, she was running with her eyes glued straight ahead, deep in thought. She didn't notice a man run by her and double back around, coming up behind her.

"Hey, long time, no see," she looked up to see Brandt's face staring at her, but she recognized Brady's voice.

"Hey, yourself. How are Eve and the kids?" she slowed her pace, eventually stopping.

"Better than ever. I didn't know you ran."

"Newly acquired habit, I guess you could say. It helps clear the mind."

"I'm glad I bumped into you. I wanted to tell you I was sorry to hear about your dad, but I'm glad he's doing alright now. And we're having a little going away party tomorrow for Bridget before she leaves for Christmas vacation. I assume you know that she has to spend two weeks with Malicious. Why don't you drop by?"

"Brady. . . I really don't think that would be a good idea."

"Is this about that big lug of a brother of mine?"

"Yeah. I think it would be a bit awkward if we were both there."

"I take it he hasn't talked to you since you've been back then?"

"Honestly, I haven't seen him since I've been back, and I hardly expect to strike up a conversation any time in the near future."

"Isn't that going to be a little difficult since you work with him, he's your neighbor, he's in your ward, he's Bridget's dad. . ."

"Not really. If things go according to plan I'll be far away from here and him," she told him. Brady was rarely serious about anything, but distress suddenly shadowed his face as though he had just realized that this wasn't just a lover's spat that was going to blow over.

"What plan?" he asked as though he were privy to her personal affairs.

"That's really none of your business, Brady. I don't have to clear anything through you," she was perturbed by his presumptiveness.

"I take it you still love him then?" Brady switched attack plans to lure more information out of her.

"What are you talking about? This has nothing to do with love. For one thing, as I recall, Brandt never once mentioned anything about loving me. For another thing, if this is what love feels like, believe me, I'm better off alone," she retorted defensively. She did not need Brady digging up the feelings she had so carefully tried to bury.

"If you didn't still love him, you wouldn't be trying to run away from him. You'd be content to stay here and make him eat his heart out as he watched suitor after suitor come to claim your hand." Brady pursued his target mercilessly.

"Funny. Guys aren't really lined up waiting to sweep me off my feet, and the only one who ever tried knocked my feet out from under me and left me to pick up the pieces," she said, letting the air out of his sail.

"Ouch."

"That's what I said after I beat myself up for being so stupid in the first place," she affirmed, but Brady wasn't one to give up so easily. He knew how to poke and prod in just the right places to extract the information he was seeking, although she was proving to be more than he bargained for.

"You know, you shouldn't be so hard on him," he had to take the cheap shot to see if his brother had any chance at rectifying this situation. Though he was acting on his own accord, he had his brother's best interest at heart.

"On him? You have got to be kidding me!" Ainsley whisper-screamed the words at him as if they could inflict the bodily harm that she wished she could unleash on him for making such a brazen comment after all she had endured the past few months. "He strings me along, then tells me he can't be with me anymore and has me transferred to Seattle for six weeks to get me out of his hair, and you're telling me not to be so hard on HIM! What on earth did I do to deserve this? Who hurt who? And another thing. I hold you personally responsible for trying to push us together in the first place!" Brady backed up a step, putting his hands up as if to show her he was unarmed.

"Whoa . . . look . . . I'm not saying he's not an idiot, which I've told him myself more than once since I found out what he did. Not that he takes much stock in anything I say because I also told him not to marry Malicious, and we see where that ended up," his face then became almost solemn looking as he continued, "Ainsley, you are the best thing that has ever happened to him, and I do mean ever, not just since the divorce. And that doesn't even include how much Bridget has blossomed since you came into her life. He didn't send you to Seattle to get you out of his hair either. I think he thought it would be easier on you after what he'd done to you, but more importantly, it was a great career opportunity."

"Well at least he was right about that," she interrupted. "Seattle is a great career opportunity: one that I hope to make permanent." There was no way Brady could sweeten the bitterness Brandt had so generously sprinkled on her crackling heart.

"Ainsley, please don't give up on him," he pleaded, defeat marching into his eyes.

"Brady, I can't force him to do what he doesn't want to do. As much as I want too, I can't even stop myself from loving him. I can't stop this grief from seeping into my heart, contaminating any hope I have for a happily ever after of my own. It's as if part of me has died. I'm just trying to learn to deal with it, and you're not helping," she explained. Brady's eyes pooled with tears, and he unexpectedly pulled her into a big bear hug. She felt tears exiting her eyes like water droplets from an automatic sprinkler. She patted his back, and he pulled away.

"I'm sorry," he said, wishing he had not launched that last missile that pierced her heart. He should have left it alone and stopped meddling in his brother's affairs. He just hated to see it end this way because there was no winner – no happiness for anyone involved.

"You know," she said, wiping away her tears, "if I had a brother, I would want him to be you. Brandt's lucky to have you."

"No, Brandt was lucky to have you," he said as he walked away.

Ainsley said goodbye to Bridget on Thursday night before she left, and despite seeing Bridget every night since she had been home, Brandt had proven himself to be a master of invisibility for which she was grateful. She didn't know exactly how she would react when she saw him or what she would say.

On Saturday evening, Ainsley was supposed to go out with Liza, Corrin, and Deedra for their last girl's night out before Liza got married. Liza suggested they dress formerly and get reservations for an upscale restaurant. When Ainsley gave herself a last glance in the mirror, she found her hair to be perfect, her make-up to be perfect, and her dress – the black one she had purchased in Seattle – to be perfect. This was going to be one of those "feel-good" nights. She felt confident and beautiful, and she liked who she saw staring back at her. She was on the rebound at last. The reflection in the mirror did not appear to be broken and sad. She had finally mastered her cover-up, and amazingly, she was looking forward to going out tonight for the first time since she had returned to Portland.

As the four friends were headed out the door, Ainsley's cell phone rang. It was her mother calling to tell her that a close family friend had died. Her mom needed some serious consoling, so Ainsley waved the others on and told them she would meet them at the restaurant. Forty-five minutes later, she hung up the phone, got in her car, turned the key, and nothing happened. She tried again and again, but to no avail.

She got out of her car, slamming the door as she said aloud, "Stupid car! Of all nights, why tonight?"

She was unaware of the presence of anyone else until he said, "Anything I can help with?" She froze with her back to him, suddenly struggling to breathe at regular intervals.

Confident. Calm. Confident. Calm. She repeated the words in her mind as she slowly turned to face him for the first time in over two months. When her eyes met his, she found them wide with surprise. He hadn't recognized her with her short hair. Surely Brady or Bridget had mentioned it to him, but he wasn't prepared for the drastic transformation in her appearance. His mouth stood slightly agape as he stared at her as though seeing her for the first time in his life. She had the upper hand for the moment.

"Expecting someone else?" she said coyly, a smile curling into place as the dimples deepened in her cheeks.

"I didn't recognize you," he muttered, though he had surely recognized the car.

"That's probably a good thing."

"Going somewhere?" he asked.

"You know, I've never given up on the nightly jog in high heels." He laughed as she spoke, shaking his head.

"And I see you still haven't taken my advice that mismatched heel lengths give you more of a workout," he quipped, and for a moment, it seemed like old times – old times she wanted back so badly she felt her resolve melting away with the sound of his voice.

"Seriously, I was going out with some friends, but I missed my ride, and my car doesn't seem to be cooperating," she explained.

"I could try to jump your car for you or give you a lift," he offered. She glanced down at her watch.

"I've probably already missed dinner by now," she said, disappointment circling her every word. "By the time I got there, they'd be ready to leave, so thanks anyway. Besides, it seems like the last time you offered your chauffer services to me things didn't end so well for either of us." Her eyes never left his, so she saw him wince slightly at her last remark.

"It looks like you had your heart set on going out. Would you mind too much if I took you to dinner?" He spoke slowly and deliberately as if he had known this exact opportunity would come if he waited long enough, but she was completely taken by surprise.

While her mind was screaming at her to say no, she heard her voice answer, "I guess you owe me at least that much."

"Just give me a minute to get ready, and I'll come back over to pick you up," he said as he walked across the grass to his porch. She called Deedra to explain what had happened while she was waiting.

"You're actually going to go out with him?" Deedra exclaimed. "Zee, that is not a good idea."

"Well, I didn't get all dressed up to sit here on my own," Ainsley responded.

"Nothing good can come of this, girl," Deedra chided.

"Deedra, I love him. My mind was screaming no, but my heart betrayed me.

It's sworn to him. It beats for him. What am I supposed to do?" She noticed Brandt emerge from his house and quickly added, "Gotta go. He's on his way over here." She hung up the phone and opened the door before he could knock.

He drove her to a nice Italian restaurant, similar to the one he had taken her to in Seattle during the training conference. There was little conversation as they drove, and the silence only seemed to deepen the gulf between them.

Before Tori worked her magic, nobody paid much attention to Ainsley when she walked into or out of any place. She simply blended in with the sea of other faces. She had been unaccustomed to people staring at her, but for some reason, tonight she was keenly aware that all eyes were on her as she was seated by the maître d'. Brandt apparently was also aware of this because he fidgeted nervously in his seat until the onlookers resumed their conversations. Ainsley felt her own jolt of nervousness. *Just a friendly gesture of reconciliation,* she told herself unconvincingly. She knew very well that Brandt still had the power to resuscitate her dying heart or to bury it for good this very night, and she wasn't quite prepared for the latter. They ordered their meal without any communication. Ainsley had never felt more uncomfortable around Brandt since her interview that day she had backed into his SUV.

"I was wrong," he admitted pointedly as she took a drink of water. She inadvertently sputtered water at him as the words registered in her mind.

"Wrong about which part?" she pressed him as he wiped the water droplets from his face.

"I was wrong to break it off how I did, wrong about Seattle. I was wrong about it all," he tried to explain, but he was merely deepening the gouge from which she was struggling to recover.

"Oh," she acknowledged coolly, unimpressed at his feeble attempt to start the inevitable conversation. She felt like he had just lit the fuse on a large piece of dynamite that was set to obliterate any hope she had of renewing their relationship. She paused for a moment, watching the spark wend its way toward the explosive. "I get it. You were wrong about me altogether. You weren't wrong to break it off, it was just how you went about it that was wrong, is that it?"

"I didn't mean it like that at all," he tried to back pedal away from his previous comment. "I was wrong to let my past influence me like I did."

"By your past, I assume you mean your ex-wife," she deduced. He nodded his concurrence.

"It was because of my reaction to her that I mistreated you in the first place, and it was because of my reaction to her that I pushed you away a second time," he admitted as the waiter brought their food to the table.

"I know you met with her in Seattle when you were supposedly at that fictitious work conference," she interjected.

"You do? How do you know that?" He was perplexed.

"Bridget told me."

"Bridget? What? How did she know?"

"Eavesdropping on a conversation between you and Brady."

"That little sneak –"

"You know Brandt," Ainsley cut him off mid-sentence, "at some point, you've got to give her some credit. You can't shield her forever. She knows when something is wrong, and you're not telling her the truth about it. Has it ever occurred to you that she doesn't need to be protected from the truth, but she needs to be told the truth so she can learn to trust again – so she can learn how to handle adversity and life in general?"

"I just don't want her to get hurt anymore," he justified.

"We all get hurt, Brandt. It's what we do with that hurt that matters – that shapes who we will become. By trying not to hurt her, you're hurting her worse.

157

She is worried and confused all the time. She just needs you to guide her through the rough patches, Brandt. You can't make them go away."

"Well, I don't think I did her any justice by turning my back on the one person she does trust: you."

"That was just a ruthless massacre of innocent souls, if you want my opinion," she said flatly.

"How can I explain this?" he said aloud, although he seemed to be talking to himself. "I'm so sorry. The words sound hollow compared to how I feel. Malissa called me to tell me she was pregnant, and I was so angry that she would dare bring another child into this world to be mistreated by her that it clouded my vision. I was scared too. The threat of my daughter being taken away from me by someone I know doesn't love her turned my world upside down. Malissa changed after she had Bridget. I never knew until it was too late that she didn't want to have kids, and Bridget suffered a lot because of it. Now, she's gone and done it again. Who knows if she wanted this one or if her birth control simply failed again. Now, she suddenly has the urge to be a mother to Bridget, although I think it has more to do with needing someone to do all of the chores and the dirty work around the house, so she suffers as little inconvenience as possible.

"I feel like I failed Bridget, but what choice do I have? I don't want to drag her through the court system and through a custody battle. Malissa has this amazing ability to get whatever she wants from whomever she chooses, so I'm betting even if I did take this through the courts, she would still be granted the same visitation to which I consented. When I got back from Seattle, I just felt like I really let Bridget down, and I guess I felt like I didn't deserve to be happy. It seems like everything I get involved with fails, so I thought I'd end it before I got too far in, well, it was already too late for that– before you got too far in. I didn't want you to get hurt too. I didn't want to suck you into my vortex, so I

158

withdrew. I know it doesn't make any sense when I try to explain it now, but for some reason it made perfect sense to me then."

"Maybe this would make more sense to you. When I saw Malissa for the first time in years at that meeting in Seattle, I came face to face with my past failures — the demons I thought I had overcome. I was overwhelmed by this sudden feeling that I could never escape my past, and anyone I included in my life would be chained to it as well. I had to free you from those chains — the chains I forged and shackled you with. You had no idea what you were getting yourself into. You deserve so much more than I can offer, so I tried to offer you the only thing I could: your freedom. Does any of this make any sense at all? I'm in uncharted waters here, and I'm not much of a sea captain."

"I don't know how to swim, so you better not sink the ship while I'm still aboard," she interjected. He laughed, feeling the tension ease between them. The waiter approached the table looking wary and confused.

"Sir, I'm sorry to interrupt, but I've had the most unusual request. The gentleman in the corner has asked that you and the lady be moved to the private table on the roof," he gestured to the corner of the dining area. Ainsley arched her neck to see who would make such an odd request, only to find Brady holding up his glass of soda in their direction as if to say, "Cheers." No wonder the waiter was confused to see that the two men were identical twins. Eve's face was beet red, and she was shaking her head in disapproval at her husband. Brandt was livid.

"I swear I did not know he was here. When I get my hands on him. . ." Brandt started to get out of his chair, but Ainsley reached across the table to push him back down.

"I think that's an excellent proposal," she said to the waiter, who immediately began clearing the table so he could escort them to the roof. "He may be meddlesome, but he has your best interest at heart," she said in Brady's defense as they followed the waiter to the roof. As they were walking, Brandt leaned toward the waiter and said, "You make sure you add the extra charge to his bill." Then he turned to Ainsley, "He'll pay for meddling one way or another."

Luckily, in the winter, the roof was enclosed and heated; otherwise, Ainsley might have thought Brady was sending them to their deaths. It was quiet without all the clanking and clattering of dishes and the muted conversations of the other guests around them. It was just the two of them, eating in silence. When they were finished, the waiter cleared their dishes, and Brandt walked to the ledge.

"Ainsley, can you ever forgive me? My life has never been darker than the day I watched you drive away. I watched, hoping you would stop the car and come back, but knowing I was the one pushing on the accelerator. When you were gone, I realized how wrong I had been. You were the key to unlocking my chains – the reason I had felt that I was finally moving forward again. If I had just taken a step back to think before I acted, I never would have made the worst mistake of my life – pushing you away. I don't want to live in the past anymore," he walked back toward her and lifted her to her feet. "Ainsley, I love you," he said. He had never in all the months they had spent together said that he loved her. Those three little words told her all she needed to hear. He had finally broken through the ranks, declaring victory over his past.

"You know, I met someone in Seattle," she admitted. He looked at the ground as she spoke. She knew it was cruel, but she couldn't help herself, so she continued, "He is really a great guy, and honestly, I don't know how I would have managed to get through those first few weeks without him. Then one Sunday, I saw you walk into church, and for one second, I thought you'd come for me. Of course, it turned out to be Brady, and I knew that you weren't coming for me. But after that, I could only see you when I looked at Dietrich, and I knew my heart could only belong to one man. Of course, it only helped your cause that he happened to be a German national who was in the United States for a short visit, so he didn't have enough time to change my mind." Brandt only half smiled at her joke, but he let out a breath of relief.

"All joking aside," she continued, "I feel as though I've been waiting for you my whole life. I know there's a reason you came into my life, and there's a reason I can't seem to get away from you or the rest of your crazy family. I feel as though God has been shuffling the puzzle pieces of my life, so they would fit together at precisely the right time. This moment is one of those pieces that just found the right spot." She leaned forward, putting her arms around his neck, and kissed him as though it were the last kiss they would ever share. It was a kiss of forgiveness, a kiss of passion, a kiss of true love, and a kiss of hope.

When she released him, she added, "There is something that has been bothering me. How did you arrange the whole Seattle transfer?"

"I'd been working on a job swap between Seattle and Portland for a while. I worked for the city of Seattle before I came here, so I had all the connections. They'd been bugging me for a while to send someone up to guide them through the integration because the department is full of new hires who are still learning the ropes, as you well know by now. We had someone else in mind, but at my insistence, Jed sent you. I'm so sorry about that too. I had no right to let my personal life affect your professional life."

"But what I don't understand is why Jed would have sent me. I have a ton of catch-up work to do, not including the fact that I now have to review all the files to make sure everything was done correctly."

"Jed is an old family friend. He and my dad go way back. I simply told him that I didn't trust anyone else to do it correctly and that if any problems did arise, you'd be the best qualified to handle them." Suddenly, Ainsley knew how a baseball pitcher felt after being hit by a line-drive as the realization struck her that Brandt was the reason she had been offered the position in the grants department in the first place. He was the reason she had been assigned to work with him on the integration project. He was behind everything, pulling the strings in his personal puppet show starring her as the marionette. He looked away sheepishly as he watched the pieces fall into place in her brain.

"You! You were behind it all. You got me the job!" As she said the words aloud, she was still struggling to comprehend it all.

"I really felt bad about that morning, and when you saw me sitting in on the interview, you looked like you'd just been sentenced to death. You were well-qualified for the position. I only cast the tie breaking vote between you and another candidate," he tried to explain while at the same time reassuring her that she hadn't been offered the job as any favor to him by Jed.

"I can't believe it. And the project?" she pressed him further to see if her assertions were accurate.

"I requested that you work with me," he admitted. "Someone from grants was going to have to be a part of the project anyway, but it wasn't meant to be a full-time thing. I convinced Jed that the project would be more efficient and effective with two dedicated analysts working on it, which wasn't a lie. It was more efficient and effective in the end."

"But why would you do that? You hated me."

"I never hated you. I admired your spunk, and I wanted to get to know you better, that's all. I was kidding around with all my sarcastic comments, but you took them as insults. I already explained that the night you accused me of attempting to 'assassinate your future.' I believe that's how you put it."

"You are unbelievable!"

"What? You're going to be mad at me now? I wasn't solely responsible for everything that happened. I didn't make you hit my SUV. I didn't have anything to do with you moving next door to me. I wasn't behind your calling as an activity day leader. I had no hand in the burglary whatsoever. And I never forced you to spend any time with me. You did that of your own free will and accord. C'mon. We just made up," he pleaded, though he didn't appear to be repentant of meddling with her career from the get-go.

"I'm not mad for heaven's sake, but I hope you can finally see that contrary to your misconception about yourself, you happen to be the source of all the positive things that have happened to me, with the exception of the last two months of course. You're the only reason I'm happy at all," she reassured him. "Who knew the chain reaction one little fender bender would cause?"

"Oh, someone knew alright. I'm absolutely convinced none of this was coincidence; it was more like divine intervention." He leaned down to kiss her again and again and again until the waiter interrupted them with the bill.

Brandt picked her up for church the next morning, and Ainsley wasn't surprised at the confused and shocked looked on the faces of the congregation. They surely must have felt as if Brandt and Ainsley were starring in their own personal soap opera. When the whispers and stares didn't cease during Sunday School, Ainsley whispered to Brandt, "Did I miss something? Why is everyone still staring?"

"They're not used to the new haircut," he whispered back while running his fingers down the back of her neck. Ainsley had all but forgotten that this was her first Sunday since her return, and nobody had seen her new look. "You really do look amazing, you know. Not that you weren't beautiful before…"

"I can't tell if their reactions are good or bad. I've experienced both, you know. My mom was less than pleased, and I've now been lowered to the likes of

Samson. Apparently, my hair was the source of my spiritual strength, and now I am but a member of the great and spacious building." Brandt burst out in laughter, interrupting the class.

"She didn't really say that to you, did she?"

"You bet. My mom's not one to mince words when she's upset. And I guess she had good reason. I purposely forgot to tell her about it because I knew what she would say. Not only was she dealing with the shock of my dad having a heart attack, but she was also envisioning her daughter as a heathen. Oh, I forgot to mention the fact that she blamed you for my downfall."

"Why not? I take it she's not happy that we are back together then, either."

"Quite the contrary. It's funny how blessings flow from our moments of trial. I would have never thought my dad's heart attack would lead to my mom's heart being softened as well, but that's how it turned out. Thanks to Bridget, that is. She sent a very timely card to my parents, and my mom's opinion of you has greatly improved. It turns out, my dad was always in your corner. He just never bothered to openly acknowledge his opinion when my mom was so opposed to us." Brandt simply smiled in response and held her hand in his.

Christmas Day was gone before she even realized it had arrived. She and Brandt spent a quiet evening alone. The best possible gift either of them could have received had already been given when they were able to reconcile, so they agreed not to exchange gifts. Brandt, however, didn't comply with the terms of their agreement because he produced a small jewelry box from under the tree. Ainsley's heart began to race in her chest until she got a closer look at the box, which was all too familiar.

"I didn't think this would count against me as getting you a gift since I've already given it to you once before," he said as he handed it to her. The green heart pendant was just as she remembered it.

"Thanks," she said. "I really missed wearing it."

"I was afraid you had written me off for good when you sent that back to me, although Bridget hid it from me for a while. You did address the package to her, you know."

"I guess meddling in people's affairs is an inherited gene in the Cragun clan," she mused.

"Yeah, I guess so," he laughed.

"I have a little something for you too," she admitted. "But I didn't break the agreement either. It was actually supposed to be your birthday present." She walked to the front door and retrieved a large, thin rectangular box from the front porch, where she had left it before she knocked on the door. He unwrapped it to reveal an elaborate pencil sketching. It consisted of nine drawings that had been varnished to a pre-made wood mat in an 18x23 inch frame. An 8x10 sketch of Brandt, Ainsley, and Bridget together was mounted in the center, and it was surrounded by 3x5 sketches, each depicting a different scene from their lives. In the upper-left corner was a sketch of Brandt holding Bridget as a baby with her head nestled in the crook of his neck. The upper-center picture was of his SUV all crunched in. The upper-right corner displayed a drawing of Bridget and Ainsley. The center-right border showed Brandt sitting at a lookout on a bench with Mt. St. Helen's in the background, while the bottom-right portrayed Brandt carrying the boy at Silver Falls with Bridget in the background. The bottom-center picture was of Brandt and Ainsley dancing, and the bottom-left hand corner was a sketch of Ainsley running alone, listening to her earbuds with a sad expression on her face.

"Did you draw this?" he asked in awe.

"Yep."

"I didn't even know you could draw."

"Just like I didn't know you could dance," she smiled.

"I guess we're both full of surprises then," he said, returning his focus to examine the pictures. "This is amazing. It must have taken forever. I can't believe how detailed and accurate the sketches are. I can even see the scar in my eyebrow. That is real talent!"

"Thanks," she said simply.

"There's only one picture I don't remember," he said, pointing to the picture of Ainsley running.

"I didn't have it quite finished before I had to leave, and I couldn't decide what I should draw for the last picture. But I wanted you to know what my life is like without you and Bridget – lonely and sad."

"Well, you never have to feel that way again. I promise you that," he assured her as he pulled her into a hug. She truly had received the first gift of Christmas – the gift of love.

The next week flew by. Brandt stayed late at work with her to help her catch up on all her grants since he had worked in the grants department in Seattle before transferring to budget and financial planning when he came to Portland. He had some church meetings to attend the night before New Year's Eve, so Ainsley spent the evening alone since Liza was now married and Corrin and Deedra had gone to Hawaii with their family for their Christmas vacation. Ainsley had just finished dinner when she heard a knock at the door. Though she hadn't been expecting any company, she was happy to see Brandt. When she told him to have a seat, however, he declined.

"Is something the matter?" she prodded.

"I just can't shake the feeling that something's not right with Bridget. While I'm not a proponent of young girls having their own cell phones, I did send her to Seattle with one, just in case. She calls me every night, and everything seems to be okay. But I've got this feeling that something bad is about to happen, and I'm three hours away. Maybe I'm just being overprotective or maybe it's because she's never been away from home before without me. I don't know," he was running his fingers through his hair in distress.

"Brandt, if you feel that strongly, I think you better heed the prompting."

"I know. I know. I've got to get to Seattle," he agreed.

"Go then. I'll still be here when you get back."

"Well, that's just it. I was hoping you'd come with me. If something is wrong, I'm going to need my anchor, so I don't drift out to sea again. And I'm not about to let you out of my sight either. Besides, I could introduce you to my parents. Wait… Brady already did that, didn't he? At any rate, they have extra rooms. Will you come with me?" She had never seen Brandt so discomposed before. His train of thought was steaming down one too many tracks at the same time, and derailment was imminent.

"It sure beats spending New Year's alone, doesn't it?"

"Great. I'll run home and pack. We'll leave in an hour," he was out the door before he finished his sentence.

Ainsley was beginning to feel as if she were going to be permanently living out of her suitcase, but she was ready to go with time to spare. She was glad she had taken New Year's Eve off as her floating holiday, so she could go with him. She could tell Brandt was unnerved the whole drive. He was nervous and restless and often so lost in his own thoughts, he didn't realize she was talking to him. Bridget called about an hour into the drive, and Brandt was encouraged by her high spirits.

"Why didn't you tell her you were on your way to Seattle?" Ainsley asked when he hung up.

"If this turns out to be nothing, I'd rather her not know. She'd drive her mom nuts begging to go to her grandma's so she could see you. She's fine, and she would definitely tell me if something was wrong. Maybe this is stupid, and I really am just overreacting."

"Brandt, you're doing the right thing, so quit worrying about it before you drive me nuts."

"Okay, okay. Let's talk about something else," he suggested, and he seemed to calm down as their conversation centered on a topic other than Bridget. They arrived in Seattle at 11:00, but his parents hadn't waited up for them. Brandt showed her to a spare room, kissed her goodnight, and disappeared down the hallway.

They slept in the next morning, and pretty much lazed about the rest of the day. Ainsley helped Betty prepare rolls and pies for dinner, while Brandt bonded with his dad in front of the television.

"We're so happy to have you here again, Ainsley, especially under more favorable circumstances this time," Betty said as she kneaded some dough. "I wanted to thank you personally for not giving up on Brandt. Of all our children, he's the one we worry about most because he tries to carry the whole world on his own shoulders."

"I've noticed," Ainsley commented as she shut the mixer off. "He would have spared us both a lot of trouble if he would have let me do my own thinking instead of trying to do it for me." Betty chuckled knowingly.

"You know I've heard it said that God answers our prayers most often through other people, and you are an answer to years of praying on Brandt's and Bridget's behalf." Ainsley realized at that moment that it wasn't only her prayers or her parents' prayers that had brought them together, but a multitude of prayers from people she hadn't even known existed. How intricately woven together are all of God's children, and how limited each of their perspectives!

"In the same sense, I could argue that he was an answer to my prayers," Ainsley replied. "Not only him, but Bridget and you and Frank and Brady and his family as well. You've made me feel like a part of the family from the very beginning in a way I never thought possible outside of my own family circle. I've never been nervous or uncomfortable around you, and that speaks volumes."

"It was just meant to be," Betty shrugged as Brandt wandered into the kitchen. Ainsley's back was turned to him as he walked over to her, slipping his arms around her waist, and nestling his head on her shoulder.

"What's meant to be?" he asked.

"You and me," Ainsley answered as he turned her around to kiss her. Betty cleared her throat.

"Oh, come on, Mom," Brandt said. "It's nothing you haven't seen before."

"That's definitely true, having raised five children," Betty agreed, "but you just backed yourself into my cherry pie filling."

"Crud," he said, examining the fresh red stain on the back of his polo shirt. "I guess that's my cue to exit." He left to change his shirt, while Ainsley and Betty resumed their cooking. They were interrupted during dinner by Brandt's cell phone. He excused himself from the table to take the call and returned a few minutes later, visibly upset.

"I knew it!" he said. "I knew she'd pull one of her little stunts. I should have never trusted her."

"What's wrong, son?" Frank asked.

"Malissa has gone to a New Year's Eve party with her husband, leaving Bridget to babysit a three-week-old baby all by herself. The baby was screaming so loud, and Bridget crying so hard, I could hardly understand what was going on."

"Good heavens!" Betty exclaimed.

"I'm going to get her right now," Brandt grabbed his car keys.

"I'm coming with you," Ainsley said as she followed him out the door.

When they got in the SUV, Brandt said, "I knew this would never work. I knew she was going to take advantage of Bridget. I blew it again. I'm going to have to take her to court now anyway," he was pounding his hands on the steering wheel in frustration.

"If you had taken her to court to begin with, you would have had no good reason for the judge not to award her joint custody. Now at least you've got something on her," Ainsley offered.

"I guess you've got a point there," he looked over at her and unexpectedly smiled – a little rainbow in the midst of a violent rainstorm. "I'm glad you're here with me." She placed her hand on his arm as he backed out of the driveway. Malissa lived fifteen minutes away from Brandt's parents. Brandt knocked on the door and walked in without waiting for Bridget to answer. He mumbled something under his breath about the door being unlocked, which only aggravated him further. Ainsley could hear a baby screaming as Bridget, her face broken out into bright red blotches from crying, flew into her dad's arms.

"Daddy!" she cried. He hugged her tightly and stroked her hair while she cried.

Ainsley went in search of the crying infant, although she wasn't exactly sure what she would do with him when she found him. He was lying on the living room floor on a blanket, screaming his little lungs out. By the looks of him, he had been born prematurely because his whole body practically fit in the palm of Ainsley's hand. He had lockets of black curly hair framing his tiny face. Ainsley found a pacifier lying on the floor next to him and tried to quiet him down by putting it in his mouth. When that failed, she checked his diaper, which was clean. Then, she went in search of a bottle as she bounced him gently in her arms on her way to the kitchen. She started to sing a Primary song as she walked, which seemed to soothe him for the time being.

Brandt was already in the kitchen mixing a bottle. He handed it to Ainsley. She would have thought the baby was nearly starved to death by the way he gulped the bottle down. She smiled as she watched him devour the milk. She had never held a brand-new baby, but was surprised at how naturally it seemed to come to her. Bridget had calmed down enough to gather her things, while Brandt collected the necessary items for the baby.

"Shoot," he said as they prepared to leave. "We don't have a car seat."

"Not to worry," Bridget piped up. "Mom left it in the garage. She doesn't like to keep it in the car when the baby isn't with her because it clashes with the interior. They just don't make car seats that match the leather," Bridget mimicked her mother's tone as she spoke the last sentence.

"You must be joking," Brandt responded. "She hasn't changed a bit." He put the car seat in his vehicle, and they headed back to his parents' house. They finished their dinner, while Betty held the baby. Even though it was New Year's Eve, Bridget was exhausted and went to bed at 9:00. Betty and Frank stayed up to watch the ball drop in Time's Square, and then they turned in as well. In the living room, Betty had already set up a bassinet, which she stored in her attic.

"You might as well go to bed too," Brandt said to Ainsley after his mother left. "It looks like it's going to be a long night with this one." The baby started to squirm on cue.

"I'll stay up with him," Ainsley volunteered. "Or maybe we could take turns with him. I'm not doing such a bad job, am I?" Brandt walked over to her and gathered her up in his arms in a hug.

"I love you so much," he said. "I've been waiting for this moment for a long time..." The baby began to cry before he could finish. Ainsley kissed Brandt's cheek.

"I'll get him," she offered as she walked to the bassinet. They took turns during the night getting up with the baby who woke up every hour and a half. They abandoned their efforts to put him in the bassinet because as soon as he left their arms, no matter how peacefully he appeared to be sleeping, he started crying. In the end, Ainsley slept with him in the rocker/recliner while Brandt slept on the couch, although Brandt got up to make the bottles when Keenan was hungry. It was the longest night of Ainsley's life, and she had pulled a few all-nighters in her college days.

"Rise and shine, sleepy head," Bridget whispered in Ainsley's ear the next morning. The baby was still snuggled in her arms, asleep. Ainsley tried to open her eyes despite their weighty objections.

"What time is it?" she asked, yawning.

"Nine-thirty," Bridget answered. Ainsley's eyes gained their focus, and she noted Brandt's absence from the couch.

"Where's your dad?" she asked.

"He got worried when mom wouldn't answer her phone this morning, so he went over to see if everything is okay."

"How long has he been gone?"

"Since seven."

"Oh, you're awake," Betty observed as she entered the living room. "Why don't you let me take the baby, and you go get something to eat and take a shower if you like?" Ainsley didn't protest as Betty gently lifted the baby from her arms. She warmed up a couple of pancakes in the microwave and then tried to wake herself up with a cool shower. At 10:30, Brandt still wasn't back, and he wasn't answering his cell phone. Ainsley looked out the window to find the SUV still in the driveway.

"He took grandpa's car. Grandpa parked behind him when he went out to get milk this morning," Bridget informed her. "Are you worried about him too?"

"I'm sure he's fine, Bridge," Ainsley tried to reassure herself as well, but she knew she couldn't just sit around and wait any longer.

"Betty, would you mind watching Bridget and the baby for a while? I've got to leave for a few minutes," she asked, and Betty ushered her out the door.

Ainsley could tell Betty was as worried as she was that Brandt had gone missing in action without calling to let anyone know what was going on. Ainsley hopped in the driver's seat of the SUV, not exactly sure of where to go. She thought about going back to Malissa's house but decided to try the pond instead. Brandt had once told her that it was his thinking spot. She parked the car and walked down the path. She knew he was there before she saw his silhouette sitting near the pond's edge. There was a slight drizzle in the air, and it was shaping up to be a cold January day. She approached hesitantly, not sure exactly what to say. Instead, she chose to say nothing as she sat down beside him. He was staring blankly into the distance beyond the pond.

"Do you ever feel like the whole world is against us?" he said quietly.

"Quite the opposite actually. There's only one person against us, and he's just holding a premortal grudge. I've always felt more like there is a magnetic force constantly drawing us together no matter how much we try to resist it," she responded, but she knew something was terribly wrong. "It must be pretty bad to provoke that comment, huh?"

"She's dead," he stated with no expression whatsoever.

"Dead?" Ainsley's echo sent a chill down her spine, and her arms erupted in goose bumps, both of which were entirely unrelated to the cold weather.

"Derrick was drunk and hit a tree around 3:00 this morning. He was killed instantly, but she died about an hour ago while I was at the hospital."

"Yikes. I certainly wasn't expecting something so drastic. Are you okay?" she put her arm around him.

"I'm ashamed because in some ways I feel relieved that she's gone – relieved that Bridget is finally free, and there won't be any court battles. But I'm also confused and angry that even in death she played the last card."

"What do you mean?"

"She asked me to be Keenan's legal guardian. I just don't understand. She has a sister who desperately wanted kids but couldn't have any of her own. When I asked about her taking him, she told me Tess was fighting a losing battle with cancer. Her parents are too old and have practically disowned her, although I find that hard to believe. She probably disowned them, since they still keep in regular contact with Bridget. They've never forgotten a birthday. Then I asked about Derrick's family, but she told me they weren't interested in taking care of any more of Derrick's wild seed – that's how she phrased it...

"I was holding her hand when she died, Ainsley. She asked me to please take care of Keenan. She begged me to promise her and had two nurses witness her sign a statement to that effect- if that's even legally binding. Her eyes were wild with fear, but it was fear for him and not herself this time, as if she really cared about him. I didn't even have time for her request to register in my mind before her hand went limp, and the monitor started sounding its alarms. I actually heard the machine signal that her heart had flat lined, and she was gone. I watched as the doctors tried to resuscitate her for twenty minutes before they pronounced her dead. And that was it. I don't even remember driving here." Tears were trickling down his cheeks, and his voice cracked as he spoke. Ainsley pulled him closer.

"I'm so sorry," was all she could say, though she knew it was of little comfort.

"I can't take care of a baby. What was she thinking?"

"Maybe she was actually thinking clearly for once. Maybe in the end, she had changed after all. You're the one person she trusted, Brandt. It seems to me that everyone else in her life ran away from her, but not you. You're the one person from whom she had to run away. Maybe that's why she never seemed to care about Bridget because she knew Bridget would always have you, and you would always take care of her. You don't seem to understand that guys like you are not easy to find. You're one in a million. You're strong. You're faithful. And when you love someone, you love them with all your heart. She knew that, and she wanted her son to feel that...to be like you. I can't blame her for that. I don't think she was trying to sabotage your life at all. I think she was trying to secure a bright future for her son."

"...but she left a brand-new baby with a ten-year-old..."

"Because she knew you would come." Brandt turned to look at her for the first time since her unexpected arrival. His eyes were no longer filled with tears, but he was staring at her so intensely she was forced to look away.

"If I knew how much one car accident would change my life..."

"I'd say," she agreed.

"I'm not talking about Malissa's. I'm referring to the day I met you, Ainsley," he turned her face so she would look at him as he spoke. "Not a moment has gone by since then that I haven't thought about you and used every excuse to see you. Even when I pushed you away. You don't know how many times I caught myself staring out my window hoping to catch a glimpse of you even though I knew you weren't there – how many times I looked for your car in your driveway when I came home, hoping you had come back – how many times I picked up the phone and dialed your number only to hang up before it rang, desperate to hear your voice – how many e-mails I composed but never sent –

175

how badly I wanted to go to Idaho to hold you and comfort you when your dad had his heart attack – how many times I've looked through that scrapbook you helped Bridget make, so for a few minutes I could see us as a happy family. I planned last night a whole lot differently. You see, I wanted to start off the new year right by telling you what I've known for a long time, but every time I tried, mom would walk into the room, or the baby would wake up…" he hesitated.

"There's no crying baby now," she observed.

"But now everything has changed. Now I have another variable to account for…"

"Brandt, why don't you tell me what you want to say, and I'll do my own accounting? I am trained in the profession, after all, and you really suck at it, if you want my opinion." He laughed.

"Before I do, may I ask you how you feel about me taking the baby if I manage to successfully navigate through all the legal hoops?"

"I think you'd be stupid," she paused as his eyes met hers. He looked as though he was suspended on a high wire waiting for her to provide the safety net just in case he faltered. "I think you'd be stupid if you tried to do it alone, that is." Having been given the green light, he proceeded.

"Ainsley, I love you. I love you more than I ever thought I could possibly love someone. I want to spend the rest of my life with you if you'll marry me," he rummaged through his jacket pocket. When he opened his palm, the diamond caught a glimmer of sunlight, flashing brightly.

"I can't believe you were nervous to ask me that, Brandt. Of course, I'll marry you!" she said.

"Do you know what you're getting yourself into? Bridget is one thing; a new baby is an entirely differently adjustment…" he asked as he put the ring on her finger.

"Do you know what you're getting yourself into?" she repeated. "You're actually going to have to just sit back, and let yourself be happy. Do you think you can handle that?" He answered with a kiss.

God was masterfully managing the intricate work of grafting their hearts together – an unlikely pair merged piece by piece, moment by moment, to produce a joy neither thought they were capable of feeling. It was a graft that healed the wounded pieces of each heart to yield two hearts beating in harmony, beating as one. Where Brandt's heart was broken, Ainsley's was whole, and where Ainsley's heart was broken, Brandt's was whole, so their hearts melded together perfectly – but not just their hearts. God was also grafting new branches into their family tree: Bridget and Keenan. From the ashes of sorrow, defeat, loneliness, and pain, a small green shoot sprang forth that cold winter day, unearthing the life and love that had been buried beneath as the ashes themselves merged into a rock-solid heart that would stand strong against any future storms.

About the Author

Tennille Jo Mortensen grew up in rural Idaho where she developed a passion for writing as she began composing poetry and short stories at a young age. After graduating with an MBA from Idaho State University, she became a full-time mother to two daughters. While focusing on her faith and family, she draws inspiration for writing from her everyday life. She enjoys hiking, photographing waterfalls, transforming socks into unique monkeys with needle and thread, and creating memories with her husband, children, and two dogs in Portland, Oregon.

Check out the Spotify playlist that inspired the author as she journeyed alongside the characters in *From the Ashes:*